Angela J. Ford

Lured by the Dusk

A Tower Knights Tale

Cover Art: Natalie Bernard

Naked Hardcover: Franziska Stern

Edits: Susan Barnes

Beware the Pied Piper
His song sweet yet sinister
Hellbent on revenge
His people to avenge
Beware your last breath
For his flute sings death

1. Tanith

Wings beat in the night sky, the sound whirring in my ears as I climbed out of my bedroom window. Jerking my gaze skyward, I narrowed my eyes, letting out a sigh as a tiny black bat flew by. A thin slice of moonlight revealed its pointed wings and red eyes. Was it an omen?

Shaking my head to dislodge my guilt, I wiggled onto the roof and used the stucco siding as a hand-hold to guide my way to the ground. It wasn't the first time I'd snuck out of the palace, but tonight, I had a dark purpose. Tonight, I planned to rob a saint's tomb.

When my feet touched the ground, I took a deep breath and scanned the area. The guards were indoors, likely drinking ale to warm themselves against the cool night and harassing the servant girls sent down to keep them company. Although no sounds of torment carried into the courtyard, I hurried across it, keeping to the shadows.

If they caught me—no, I wouldn't think about it. The bruise on my stomach had only just healed from the last time I'd displeased my uncle, Lord Faren of Dowler. He'd punched me so hard I couldn't breathe without pain for two days, leading up to my decision to stop just thinking about escape and to take action. The side gate was ajar, just as I'd left it earlier, and I slipped out, following the path toward the graveyard.

The walk would be faster on horseback, but the noise would alert the night watch, which ensured the citizens of Dowler stayed indoors after curfew. My chief concern wasn't being caught by the guards, or my room being discovered empty—for after a few unsavory incidents, I'd gotten wise and started to lock it each night. No, my primary worry was what lay in the graveyard and whether the rumors about monsters were true or false.

The half-moon sulked behind a cloud, making the night more eerie. A breeze kicked up, cold like dead fingers, forcing me to pull my cloak tighter around my neck. Even though it was only late summer, the mountain air always held a bite, making me long for the warmth of Solynn. Tonight's theft would allow me to return to the city where everything had gone wrong. What I'd do once I arrived, I wasn't sure, but one step at a time. I had to focus on tonight's plan and unravel the future once I escaped this cursed place.

The graveyard was a plot of land near the outskirts of the city, and I was out of breath by the time I arrived. I slowed, searching for signs of life.

"Tanith?" came a low murmur.

"Carter?" I whispered back, my scalp prickling as I neared the field of death. My accomplices had come, which meant there was no turning back now.

"We're here," he confirmed.

I climbed over the low stone wall and pulled back the cowl of my cloak. A lantern sat in the overgrown grass, giving off a small pool of light, enough for me to see the faces of the orphaned brothers who worked in the palace: Carter, a lean youth of about twenty and his seventeen-year-old brother, Kinder. Carter was smitten with me, and it hadn't been difficult to persuade him to assist me tonight, while Kinder followed along because he was a bit slow and easily intimidated.

I tugged at the clasp of my cloak, chest tight, as we huddled together. If caught, I'd be subjected to a lecture from my aunt, Lady Matzie of Dowler, and some violence from my uncle, but Carter and Kinder, as mere servants, would be severely punished. I'd never forgive myself if I were the reason they were beaten.

"We shouldn't be doing this." Kinder's voice quavered.

"We'll be quick," I reassured him, for I had no desire to linger among the departed souls any longer than necessary. Superstition held it was bad luck to disturb the dead, but considering my uncle's violence, the blood rituals at the temple, and the scent of rot that wafted up from somewhere beneath the palace, I'd take my chances with the dead. "Carter, can we get into the mausoleum?"

Carter's voice surged with pride. "I stole the keys from the groundskeeper two nights ago and he didn't even notice."

Mouth dry, I turned back to Kinder. "Stand watch. If anyone comes, hoot like an owl and disappear."

"I will, but hurry. It's creepy out here," he fretted.

I nodded in agreement. We could not get caught. If we heard anything odd, we were supposed to run in different directions and disappear as quickly as possible. If anyone was out, they'd assume it was the spirits haunting the graveyard. At least, that was the hope.

"I brought shovels in case we need to dig up

anything," Carter said. "And here, I have extra candles."

His fingers were rough but steady as they brushed mine. I tucked the candles into my pocket, determined to do this with steely courage. The dead did not need the relics they were buried with. We did.

"Let's go," I told him.

We crept through the long grass to the mausoleum, a small building in the heart of the graveyard, carved with glyphs and guarded by statues to honor Saint Dowler, for whom the city was named. He'd founded it hundreds of years ago by cutting a path through the mountains and using the surrounding river to make it prosperous. The citizens treated Saint Dowler like a god and even left offerings for him during the turn of each season to ensure continued blessings and wealth.

Rumor had it that when he died, the people had buried a portion of his wealth with him, which was why the mausoleum was kept under lock and key. But an aura of fear surrounded the graveyard, and I often wondered why the tomb of a saint who was so revered was on the outskirts of the city instead of behind the temple, where my uncle's family line was buried.

Three steps led up to the door, and Carter

pushed his shoulder against it, the sound of stones scrapping against each other loud in the silence. Stale air assaulted my senses and a sudden panic clawed up my throat, making me long for the fresh night air. Pressing a hand to my stomach, I forced myself to step inside. If we succeeded—no, *when* we succeeded—I'd finally be free of my uncle's violence and the threat of hidden corruption that laced the palace. This would be over soon. I could stave off my panic long enough to finance my return to Solynn.

"Here." Carter passed me one of the shovels.

A moment later, a torch flared, casting a pale glow around us. Just inside, a set of stairs led into darkness. Goose bumps went up my arms as Carter led the way down, holding up the light. I could feel the cold stone even through my shoes, as if death were seeping through the rock, trying to find me. When we reached the bottom, a sense of foreboding passed over me, making it difficult to forget about the supposed curses that haunted those who disturbed the dead.

"Look," Carter said. His voice wobbled, making him sound both younger and smaller.

He waved the torch, allowing us to see the sloped walls and the empty space ahead. My throat tightened.

"Wait, this can't be right." Where was the elaborate tomb with offerings stacked around it?

Shifting the shovel to my other hand, I grabbed the torch from Carter and stepped further into the open space, my scalp prickling. There had to be another layer to the tomb. But why go through all the trouble of building a large crypt when St. Dowler was the only one buried here?

And then I saw it, a narrow passage leading downhill into darkness. I marched toward it, Carter following somewhat reluctantly behind me. The flickering flame revealed frescos painted on the stone. I longed to stop and decipher their meanings, but time was of the essence.

A slight wind came out of nowhere as I stepped into an open space and held the torch up high. A silver glimmer came from the middle of the room, growing brighter as we approached.

"Oh." Awe stole my voice as I spun slowly. This was what I had expected.

Stone columns and arches towered above me, and the torch light caught on openings, a labyrinth of passageways that led deeper into the crypt. A coffin sat on a dais, so high that a set of stairs led up to it. Atop the coffin was the glowing, silver prism, but my eyes were drawn to the treasure surrounding it: old books covered in cobwebs, pottery so coated in dust it was hard to tell whether it was worth anything, weapons covered in rust, statues of hideous beasts—jewelry hanging off their necks and arms—and precious stones scattered like pebbles in the road.

Relief made my knees weak. Leaning the shovel against the wall, I put the torch in one of the two holders by the door. It only cast a small pool of light, but it was enough as I opened my satchel and moved to the treasure.

I expected a low whistle of surprise from Carter, but when I glanced over my shoulder, he stood rigid at the entrance to the room. Impatience snapped around me. "Come on, we have little time," I hissed.

Carter's face was pale, a sheen of sweat shining on his brow. He licked his lips and shook his head. "Kinder was right, this is wrong."

"You weren't afraid when we planned this," I scoffed. My words sounded brave, but I had to admit, a sacred aura hung in the air. Would I be cursed if I stole from a dead saint?

"I know, but now that we're here, I see this is wrong. The dead need their gifts for the afterlife and if we steal from them, especially from a saint, there will be consequences."

I crossed my arms and sighed, wanting to lash out, but knowing it would only drive Carter away. He was a sweet boy, and he'd only gone along with the idea to please me. Putting on my best coaxing tone, I tried to persuade him. "We're already here. The hard part of sneaking out and not getting caught is over. We just have to grab the treasure and then we'll leave."

Shaking his head, Carter stepped back. "This isn't right. We need to leave. Now."

I frowned, trying to ignore the ball of anxiety that lay in the pit of my stomach. When I closed my eyes, I recalled the smack of a fist against my flesh, and the pain that rocked through my core. It was all the motivation I needed. With a sigh, I gave in. "Go, stand guard with Kinder. I won't be long."

"I'm sorry, Tanith," Carter apologized.

Spinning on my heel so I wouldn't see him leave, I marched toward the treasure. I did not want to be alone in the tomb, but if I moved quickly, it should only take a few minutes. I could handle some momentary discomfort to finance my escape. Opening my satchel, I stuffed in jewelry and as many coins as possible. When I reached Solynn, I'd go to a jeweler to determine the true value of these treasures. My fingers danced over the thick books and fat scrolls that lay on the steps. If I had more time, I would have loved to read them. Surely the saint had possessed ancient wisdom and knowledge, although why these books were buried with him I could not fathom.

The flame of the torch flickered, reminding me that time was running out. My gaze moved to the coffin and the silver glow hovering above it. That ball of dread inside tightened and as I reached for more treasure, pain lashed across my skin. Sucking in a deep breath, I jerked my palm to my chest. Looking down, I realized I'd inadvertently picked up a knife. Even though the years should have dulled the blade, a river of blood dripped down my hand and my pulse pounded as I waited for the initial pain to subside.

A far off sound drifted to my ears, a faint call like the hoot of an owl. I froze, whipping my head around to the entrance, where the torch burned even lower. I licked my lips. Someone was coming. Forgetting about my wound, I leaped to my feet, knocking over pottery. It fell with a crash, sending shards of broken clay flying across the floor. A pile of coins came loose and slid down the steps. In the silence, the noise was terrifying, and a whimper came from my lips. I'd stolen enough. Time to go.

But as I moved, the silver prism winked, capturing my vision. Somehow it had fallen off the coffin and was perched on the first stair, merely a foot above me, as though it wanted me to take it. I hesitated. The object was an artifact that belonged in the tomb, but it was a rare find. If I didn't take it, I'd regret it. Besides, it might be worth enough to give me back the life I'd had before my parents died, before I was forced to come to Dowler.

I made up my mind in a flash and lunged for it. My fingers closed around its cold, hard mass, the blood on my fingers making it slippery. I cupped it in my hands and blew across the surface. Dust danced away like a cloud and the silver glow turned blue. A comfortable warmness flooded through my skin and a sense of peace came over me as I held the prism.

No, it was a pyramid, made of crystal and heavy in my palm. Inside, the glow came from a rock suspended at the top. Below it was a collection of obsidian stones, flakes of gold, and some sort of design. Were those words? I peered closer, brushing my finger over the top. My blood smeared on it, a reminder that I needed to leave and bandage my cut. I could examine the stolen treasures later.

Dropping the pyramid into my satchel, I started toward the exit, but the ground beneath my feet shook. I glanced back at the coffin, now dark without the pyramid's light. Maybe my movements had disturbed something. Mouth dry, I considered all the passageways, stretching out into who knows where. There were no signs of life aside from myself in the crypt, but something malevolent might dwell here.

Taking a deep breath to calm my rising panic, I broke into a run, but the tremor came again, halting my forward momentum. Holding out my arms to steady myself, I walked, hoping the slower pace would help me keep my balance, but the shaking increased until it felt like the beginning of an earthquake. I lost my balance and landed heavily on my side.

Coins spilled from my satchel. Cursing, I scrambled on all fours to snatch them up. The shaking continued, making my teeth rattle in my skull. I worked quickly, crawling closer to the nearest passageway until the torch lost its perch and fell, plunging me into utter darkness.

I hissed as cool threads of fear gathered around me and the shaking stopped. Shakily, I rose to my feet, hands reaching for the candle and flint that should be in my pocket, when hands locked around my waist and yanked me backward.

2. Tanith

"Carter, let go," I snapped, fear edging my tone.

The arm around me tightened, and a masculine voice vibrated through me. "Who is Carter?"

Bile rose in my throat. I kicked out and waved my arms, desperate to escape as terrible thoughts swam through my mind. I had not heard anyone enter the crypt, but what if the spirits were real? What if they'd come alive? What horrors would they inflict on me?

The man or spirit did not speak again as I fought him. I threw back an elbow, which connected with something solid, and kicked, my heel smacking into a leg. He merely grunted and redoubled his efforts to subdue me, his arm around my waist so tight it was bruising.

I gasped for air, my heart pounding in my ribcage as I scratched the arm holding me, digging in with my short nails as best I could. The man lifted me off my feet and I jerked my head back. Hard. I heard a snap and he finally dropped me. I tumbled to the ground, crying out as I landed on the broken shards of pottery. Ignoring the cuts, I crawled on all fours as fast as I could. This was a nightmare, worse than what I'd feared when I entered the crypt. Someone else was here, someone who might kill me if I didn't escape.

The shovel. If I could reach it, I could bash him in the head and run, even though it was impossible to see in the dark. Gathering some of the sharp pottery shards as a weapon, I continued to crawl forward, but a hand clamped down on my ankle, forcing me to stop. I kicked out but missed as he dragged me backward, my body scrapping painfully across the floor. He flung me on my back and a weight settled on me, pinning me down. One hand caught my arms, dragging them above my head, and the other hand clamped down over my mouth and nose.

I thrashed and bit, arching my body to knock him off me, trying to clamp down on his skin. But it was to no avail. The man was much stronger than me and his hold stayed firm. I struggled for air, my attempts at escape growing weaker and weaker. This was the end. I should have left, like Carter suggested. The treasure was cursed, and this was my punishment for stealing.

I MUST HAVE PASSED OUT, for when I awoke, the grave robbery seemed like only a nightmare. At first, I assumed I was back in my lavish room, about to awaken to a tongue lashing from my aunt's maid, Uropa. I'd lost my title and wealth after my parents' death, but my aunt and uncle still expected me to act like a lady, with a meek disposition and elegant manners, smiling at potential suitors, whether or not they were twice my age.

Fortunately for me, my parents had raised me to seek knowledge, ask questions, and maintain my independence. Unfortunately, their deaths had forced me to rely on the only family I knew, my aunt and uncle, the Lord and Lady of Dowler. I'd heard nothing but vague stories about the wealth of the mountain city they ruled over, for my father refused to discuss his older brother. My aunt sent for me after my parents died and at the time, I assumed Dowler would be a safe place to grieve. Now, I wished I'd never come.

Opening my eyes, I sat up and gray stone tilted beneath me. It hadn't been a dream. The clean air was the first sign, slightly musty. I blinked, frowning at a fire in the hearth. Tiny flames licked at the wood as if it had just been lit. The floor beneath me was filthy. Gray cobwebs hung from the ceiling and odd lumps surrounded me. It took me a moment to realize it was furniture, covered with cloth. I gaped, my mouth opening and closing as I tried to work out where I'd ended up.

Shakily, I rose to my feet, and a voice floated out of the silence. "You're not going to run, are you?"

It was the same masculine voice I'd heard in the tomb, and I whipped around. Amber eyes bored into mine. My breath hitched as I took in the man. No, not a man, for he had pointed ears that poked through a mane of fox-red hair that fell to his shoulders. His eyebrows were arched, his face a painful display of perfection and arrogance—full lips, aristocratic nose, high cheekbones. Warmth filled my cheeks at his state of undress. A once white shirt was open, displaying an expanse of hard, muscled chest. His sleeves were ruffled and his trousers were far too tight, too short even. Was this the man who assaulted me in the tomb?

"Who are you? Where am I?" I demanded breathlessly, eyes darting across the small room. If I snatched a burning branch from the fire and tossed it at him, would it give me enough time to escape?

His lips parted in a feral grin and his nostrils flared, as though he sensed my desire to flee and it awakened a wolfish need to hunt. Jeweled eyes narrowed as his gaze raked over my body. "I caught you, little thief, so you're going to explain your actions, and I'll decide a fitting punishment for your crimes."

Punishment. I gulped and scanned the room again. He had his back to the door and the windows were high. If I broke through one, would I land on the ground? In water? It was hard to tell how far up we were. I peeked at the man who watched me with a chilling expression, which turned harder as he glanced at the fire and then the windows.

"We're in my castle. There is no escape," he said bluntly.

I clutched my cloak in my fists, determined to show no fear. Jutting my chin out, I demanded. "Who are you? Not the groundskeeper, I've seen him. How do I know you weren't robbing the tomb too? No one was supposed to be down there."

A muscle in his jaw twitched, and a smirk covered his face. He held something in his hands, which glimmered. It took me a moment to realize it was the strange pyramid I'd taken. Even from a distance, it sparkled with a beauty that made my stomach twist.

My fingers twitched with the desire to snatch it from him, but a flash of white pulled my gaze back to my hands. A bandage covered the cuts on my palm. I drew in a sharp breath and glared at the man.

"No, I'm not the groundskeeper," he confirmed. "I was sleeping peacefully in my coffin, and you woke me up." He held up the pyramid. "With this."

A numbing sensation of terror swept over me. "You're the ghost of Saint Dowler," I breathed, despite the fact he did not look like a spirit. Then again, I'd never seen one before. Perhaps spirits didn't look like wisps of whiteness. Maybe they looked alive, like he did. Although I couldn't image how his flesh hadn't rotted.

He smiled, showing off a neat row of canine-sharp teeth. I shivered. The idea of jumping out the window sounded better than facing him for much longer.

"I'm no saint, but it's ironic you would think so. The tomb was built to keep me in, to ensure I never woke to cause chaos or chase retribution again. The ruse was to pretend it was the tomb of a saint, to pile it with offerings—gifts, treasure—all to hide the keystone, a way to awaken me. A secret, hidden in plain sight." He chuckled darkly. "And you, my bold thief, entered my sacred crypt, took my treasure, and woke me up. Wouldn't you agree you owe me?"

My lips trembled as my breath caught. Suddenly, I understood why the graveyard was on the outskirts of town and the rumors that surfaced about it. It had all been a hoax to keep everyone out, perhaps even the reason for the curfew. Did Lord Faren know the truth and keep the citizens in the dark? This situation was very wrong, yet the horror that consumed me wasn't born out of surprise, but the awareness that something awful like this would happen in Dowler.

"I'm sorry," I whispered, deciding it was best to grovel and apologize. I'd never been one for tears, but now I wished I could force them from my eyes to try and soften his hard heart. "It was wrong of me to steal from you. I'll give everything back."

He snorted. "I took the liberty of emptying your pockets while you slept."

I stepped back, pained at the thought of him going through my pockets while I lay unconscious. But he had taken the time to bandage my hand which had to mean he didn't want to kill me. "Will you allow me to go home?"

"Home? Where is home for a pretty thief like you? The gutter? A dark alleyway? Perhaps an empty house, the owners dead and rotting."

A bolt of anger sizzled through me at his taunting words, and I found my tongue again. "No, if you must know, I live in the palace where the Lord and Lady of Dowler dwell."

He went rigid and ceased tossing the pyramid. A strange look crossed his face, eyes glinting with … greed? Giving me a wolfish grin, he stepped forward. "Tell me, how much time has passed? Who rules Dowler now?"

I had his attention. "My uncle is Lord Faren and my aunt, Lady Matzie."

"Ah, and you grew up here?"

"No." I bristled. "I'm from the city of Solynn. I only came here two years ago, after the death of my parents, and I was only robbing your tomb for passage back to the city."

"An orphan. Why would you want to leave Dowler?" He asked, eyes gleaming with curiosity.

I scowled. "For personal reasons, namely because it's hellish here."

"Hellish," he repeated. "That's a word I haven't heard in a while."

I rolled my eyes. Well, of course not, he'd been sleeping. In a coffin. I expected he'd heard little, but I bit my tongue to keep the retort from falling out of my mouth. Hugging myself, I tried my best not to glare at him as I shifted closer to the fire. It was drafty in the room and the fire hadn't been burning long enough to chase the chill away.

"Do you know who I am?"

I scowled at him, since I'd asked him twice and he hadn't seen fit to respond. Until now. Part of me wanted to slap the smirk off his angelic face, but the other part of me was still turning over the term punishment, and what he might do to me when the conversation ended.

"Some have called me the Devil of Dowler, but I'm better known as the Piper."

Devil. Piper. My entire body trembled. My actions tonight had been desperate, and now I'd awakened the Devil of Dowler. I shook my head so hard my curls tumbled around my face. "No, no, no," I whispered as I backed away from him. "It's not possible. You're just a scary story, a fable told to keep children from misbehaving or going too deep into the forest. You can't be real."

Distaste crossed his face as he stepped closer to me. When he spoke, his voice was a low warning, exactly the dark timbre I'd expect from the devil.

"I'm the Devil of Dowler and you trespassed, which means you're mine."

His hand shot out, and I half expected horns to sprout from his head and claws to appear in place of his fingers. A scream stuck in my throat, begging to escape. Instead, I lunged for the fire, snatched up a piece of flaming wood and tossed it at him. Shaking my burning fingers, I fled.

3. TANITH

During the first month of my stay in Dowler, I remarked to Uropa about the beauty of the city—the wealthy citizens, the fresh mountain air, the bright flowers that bloomed by the river, and the overall picture of health and happiness. She'd stared at me with disapproving eyes, and, thinking back, inwardly she must have been laughing at my stupidity. "Let me tell you a story."

I'd perched on the windowsill, raising an eyebrow. "A true story?"

"Decide for yourself after I finish."

"Alright," I'd agreed.

"Hundreds of years ago, when the city of Dowler was still a floundering civilization, an odd man who called himself the Piper appeared. The citizens were unkind to him because of his strange looks, unusual habits, and the way he played his flute. He kept to himself in the woods outside the city, and those who went to play tricks on him never came back the same, if at all. Whispers circulated that he had the power to control minds with his flute, but since no one could prove it, nothing happened.

"One day, the city was struck with a plague from the northern reaches. Famine destroyed the crops, farm animals died, and even the river dried up until one could walk in and pick up the fish from the riverbed. Sickness was next. The children fell ill with a terrible cough, and soon it passed to the women and men. Dowler was on the brink of failure and everything that had been built was about to be destroyed. But along came the Piper.

"He walked out of the woods, playing his magic flute. The music coaxed the skies to open and brought heavy rains down on the land. The fields sprouted, the flowers bloomed, the animals revived, and best of all, those who were sick rose the next morning, healthy, hungry and strong.

"The people rejoiced and praised the Piper, who went to the Lord of Dowler for his reward. But they cast him out and asked him to return to his abode in the forest, for his power was unnatural. Disgraced and unwanted, the Piper took his revenge by enacting a series of terrors. People died under mysterious conditions, children disappeared, wolves attacked those who went out at night. Anyone who went into the woods to hunt down the Piper never returned. Until one day, the Lord of Dowler found a source of magic and made the Piper disappear."

"And then what happened?" I asked.

Uropa shrugged. "That's it, but the tale has shifted throughout the years. Some say if you go into the woods, you'll hear his flute and lose your wits searching for it. Legend holds that if you find him, the Piper will force you to do his bidding."

I laughed out loud. "Do you believe this?"

Uropa turned back to her work. "It's part of the history of Dowler. Laugh all you want, but everyone knows the tale."

And then she repeated a refrain, one that danced in my mind long after she'd left.

Beware the Pied Piper
His song sweet yet sinister
Hellbent on revenge
His people to avenge
Beware your last breath
For his flute sings death

I BOLTED into a musty hall with pools of flickering candlelight. Unable to guess where the exit might be, I picked a direction at random and ran.

I did not get more than a few feet when a weight landed on my back, knocking me down. I fell with a grunt, limbs flailing as he effortlessly flipped me on my back, pinning my legs with his thighs and holding my arms with his hands.

"You shouldn't have run," he hissed, those sharp teeth mere inches from my face.

"You're the devil. I had to try," I retorted, fury overriding my fear.

He clicked his tongue behind his teeth. "You'll learn," he whispered, as if he wasn't even talking to me. Louder, he added. "A shame, since I was considering taking you home."

Home. Yes. It's what I wanted. I held my breath, unable to look away from his penetrating gaze. His weight on my body was stirring up sensations better left alone, and I wanted him to move. When he bared his teeth, my breath caught and something I could not explain happened. His amber eyes glazed as he bent nearer to me, his nose close to my neck, as if he were breathing in my scent.

The Piper of Dowler held me down, and instead of fighting, I lay there and let him bring his teeth close to my neck. I swallowed hard, struggling against the temptation that grew within, a rash decision ready to cloud my mind. Again. Sometimes I sabotaged myself with my impulsiveness and now was such a moment. In the low light, I inhaled, aware of the male body rising above mine. This was inappropriate. Wrong. And yet a stir of something that wasn't fear rose with me as his breath kissed my bare skin and his teeth sank into my neck.

It was just a nip, not hard enough to draw blood, and yet enough to jolt me out of my hazy thoughts. Was the Devil of Dowler trying to seduce me? "What are you doing?" I demanded, bucking underneath him, which was a mistake. It only made him clasp me tighter as his wicked eyes skated over my face, lingering on my lips.

A bolt of carnal lust went through me again. Why wasn't my brain working? I should be screaming, begging, not thinking of furious kissing.

"Give me your name," he coaxed, as if he hadn't just tried to taste me.

"Tanith." I spoke between clenched teeth.

"Tanith," he purred. "I don't trust you. Give me a reason I shouldn't tie you up and take you home."

I bit my lower lip, heart racing. This was it? He would not punish me? "If you're taking me home, I promise not to run. But ..."

He arched an eyebrow. "You have a question?"

"Yes. No. You don't have to come with me."

"Mm. It would be reckless of me to leave you alone in the woods. The creatures that roam at night will not hesitate to take what they desire."

It sounded as though he were warning me about himself, not other nocturnal beasts. "Shall we go then?" I asked, hoping he'd get off me.

"In a hurry to escape my lair?"

"I snuck out," I admitted. "I don't want anyone to see me sneak back in."

"Ah, a resourceful little thief."

He sprang to his feet, catching me by the arms and pulling me up. As soon as he let go, I stepped away, eager to put distance between us.

Darkness shrouded the halls as he led the way, the candles lighting as we near and extinguishing themselves when we'd passed. Magic. I would have been enchanted if I hadn't been worried about whether the Piper would remember his so-called punishment. But he seemed to forget about it as we walked side by side, our arms occasionally bumping.

I wanted to add more distance, but didn't want to give him any reason to change his mind.

Tight-lipped and silent, we left his castle, stumbling out into pine-scented air and rows of trees, branches overhanging the path like claws, twisting away to who knew where. It was only as we left the courtyard behind that I wondered if he was truly taking me home, or just to another place deep in the forest where he could peel the flesh from my bones and hide the evidence.

A tic of fear bubbled up, but I repressed it, turning my thoughts to Carter and Kinder. Had they escaped? The treasure would have helped them leave Dowler and start somewhere new, but now they were just as stuck as I was. That bitter thought stung like needles. Tonight was supposed to be my great escape from the abuse of Lord Faren.

The first time he'd hit me was when I'd decided to explore the vast palace. It had more rooms and layers than I could count. I'd found my way down, somewhere where the sunlight did not shine, to a curious set of double doors which vibrated. I'd walked up to them, admiring the intricate design—swirls of vines and flowers, and what looked like waves. My uncle had come out of nowhere, fingers digging into my arm as he dragged me away. "You're not supposed to be down here," he growled.

"I was just exploring," I'd retorted.

That's when the slap came, cutting across my cheek like white fire, so intense I flinched back.

"You will speak to your elders with decorum. Now don't let me catch you down here again."

And that was only the beginning of my insight into his temper. There were more areas off limits than I could count and no explanation why. In my parents' house, I'd been free to come and go as I pleased, and they'd kept no secrets from me. In Dowler, I was a nuisance, even more so because I was the past the marrying age, and my aunt and uncle wanted to secure a match so I'd no longer be a burden. I wasn't worried about marriage. I just wanted to be in control of my life again.

4. Tanith

The Piper caught my hand and tucked it under his elbow, ensuring he had a firm hold on me. Not that I planned to run away. The woods were black and spooky under the ghost-like glow of the fading moon, which threatened to sink behind another clump of clouds. My mind raced, trying, failing, to make a plan in case things went wrong with this demented man. Not a man. Piper. Spirit?

Putting two fingers to his mouth, he gave a low whistle. A brief silence hung in the air, followed by the distinct pounding of hooves galloping over ground. I squeezed the Piper's arm as the beast came into view. Not the horse I expected, if it was a horse at all. The beast trotted up to us, with a black mane, red eyes glowing and skeletal wings tucked on its back. It snorted, white teeth flashing, and my limbs went weak. Could this night get any worse? Clearly, the Piper expected me to ride on a demon horse. I'd rather walk the miles back to the palace.

It was too late to run, and the Piper dragged me with him, wasting no time in greeting the horse as he swung up, hauling me behind him. The bone-white wings spread out, but instead of taking flight, the horse reared up on its back legs. Giving a deep-throated cry, that sounded more like a growl and nothing like what a horse should sound like, it galloped into the night.

Usually, I enjoyed riding on horseback, especially with the wind blowing past me. Tonight, I held tight to the Piper. Even though I sat astride, the lack of saddle left me feeling as if I could slip off the horse's back, crash to the forest floor and shatter every bone. Left to die, I'd be consumed by the wildings in the wood, and that was not the fate I had in mind for myself.

Wind tore at my eyes and yanked at the loose threads of my hair. My cloak billowed out behind me and icy air seeped in from each angle. Except from the Piper. He was warm, alive, and I held tighter to anchor myself to reality.

When we reached the city, the horse slowed its deathly gallop to a more reasonable pace, hooves clopping over the paved street. I stifled a cry of fear, my mind going to the curfew that insisted everyone be indoors two hours before midnight. Now, everyone would hear the horse trotting down the street.

My anger returned, and I straightened up. "You'll wake everyone with this racket."

"What are you afraid of?" The Piper tossed the words over his shoulder.

A gust of wind stole my retort and hurled it into the street.

The Piper chuckled at my lack of response, as though he controlled the wind, just like the fable claimed. My anxiety rose as the palace loomed ahead, carved out of a great mountain to frown down upon the people of the city and remind them who was in control. High iron gates surrounded the palace, and attached to it was the temple, where the priests conducted their blood rituals.

Earlier, I'd taken the side gate, meant for guards to sneak in and out unseen if the city were ever under siege. But now, the Piper thundered toward the main gates, and my chest squeezed. How was I supposed to sneak inside with him awakening the city? If Lord Faren found out what I'd done, I'd be laid up in my bed, recovering for at least three days, if not more.

When the main gates appeared before us, I yanked on the Piper's shirt. "The gates are locked!"

Instead of heeding my warning, he proceeded. The horse reared up, hooves striking against the iron with a loud, ringing sound. I cried out, squeezing the Piper's waist as the gates opened with a bang. A ripping and tearing followed as we galloped into the courtyard, leaping over bushes and statues all laid out in a particular design by the gardeners.

My heart rushed, thudding harder. When I glanced behind us, the carnage was worse than I expected, the gates hanging on by a hinge. "By the gods!" I sputtered, a sinking sensation stirring in my gut.

The Piper had no regard for anyone or anything, and I'd been so concerned about getting home, I hadn't considered what might happen once I arrived.

We galloped to the stairs leading inside, and the horse barely stopped before the Piper swung down, dragging me with him.

"What do you think you're doing?" I hissed as he took my elbow and escorted me to the palace entrance.

The doors opened at his touch, as if they hadn't been locked, and we entered the grand hall, but we weren't alone.

Lord Faren strode toward us, appearing as if he'd

tumbled out of bed and tossed his royal robes on, but even with his ruffled black hair, he cut an imposing figure. Fury lined his face, and his deep-set eyes were red rimmed as he glared, first at me, and then at the Piper. Something in his dark gaze flickered, and regardless of the guards surrounded him, I thought I caught a hint of fear.

"What is the meaning of this?" he bellowed.

The silence that followed was deafening, and I knew I'd made an awful, terrible mistake.

Just as I expected, the noise from the horse had awakened everyone. Lords and ladies in their nightdresses gathered, as well as sleepy-eyed servants, and guards without their livery and armor, swords held in hand. The hall filled as they came, curious and expectant, and the Piper stared at each of them and grinned, showing off his row of wicked teeth.

Flinging out his free arm, he announced. "Has everyone gathered? If so, we can begin."

I scanned the crowd for a friendly face, my heart sinking. Since I'd come to Dowler, I'd been the oddity, the one who was too curious, who wouldn't dress like a lady, or sit at dinners, charming the lords and entertaining the ladies. Now, I'd appeared in the middle of the night, breaking curfew and bringing the devil to their doorstep.

When I locked eyes with my aunt, she whispered

to Uropa. Aunt Matzie had never been unkind to me, nor had she been very warm. She and my uncle had three children—ages five, seven, and nine—and she spent most of her time with them, leaving her little energy for anyone else. Sometimes I wondered if my uncle had driven all the fight out of her with his quick temper. If I'd had to endure punches and slaps, what had she endured as his wife?

Uropa wove her way through the crowd, quickly disappearing while I took a step away from the Piper. But he held my arm and yanked me right back, so hard I almost lost my footing. Determined not to embarrass myself further, I lifted my chin. Let them look, let them see me covered in grit and dust, escorted by a dangerously attractive man who wasn't human. Giving him a side-eyed glare—which he ignored—I wondered if he had a name.

Lord Faren bristled, and when he spoke next, the anger in his tone was laced with authority. "Why are you here with my niece?"

I noticed he did not address me at all, and his words insinuated something more, as though I'd been sneaking out to rendezvous with the Piper to conduct illicit deeds. I was no innocent maiden, but I flushed hot at the very idea, and suddenly, I was reminded of his teeth on my neck.

"It's a bit of a story," the Piper began lightly, as if

a furious lord and guards with swords did not surround him. "I was sleeping, rather peacefully, in that grave your ancestors tossed me in. You're Lord Faren I assume, which makes you which generation? The third or fourth since the people were conned into believing a benevolent saint was buried in the crypt?"

"Speak plainly," Lord Faren snapped.

"Oh, but I am, and you will want to listen to this next part very carefully. I was asleep until a thief entered the crypt to steal my treasure. You would agree that stealing is a crime and deserves a punishment, no?"

"Bring me this thief and I will punish him myself!"

"Hm, besides the crime of stealing, this thief also woke me up."

My uncle's gaze flashed to me, and his eyebrows lifted. Wordlessly, he took in my cloak and the smudges of dirt on my clothing. Instead of dropping my gaze, I boldly stared back, defying him. Aware I'd pay for it later.

"As it turns out, your niece is the thief, and since she trespassed and stole from me, I shall decide her punishment. Because of her actions, in accordance with the treaty, I may make an additional request."

What treaty, and why was Lord Faren listening to

this instead of tossing him out? I wanted to interject, but a palpable tension hummed in the air. I'd already done enough tonight.

"The treaty stands," Lord Faren said. "Make your request, so we might all be done with this interruption and go back to bed."

I tried, once again and unsuccessfully, to pull away from the Piper. When he tightened his grip on my arm, the sinking sensation doubled. He'd mentioned punishment. Was this what he had in mind? To bring me back and embarrass me in front of everyone who lived in the palace?

"I hoped you might agree," the Piper said with a hint of malice in his tone. "My request is that your sorcerers free the magic-thralls, and don't pretend you know nothing about them. Lies will not appease me, and I smell the taint of magic that courses through your city like a river."

Magic-thralls?

I studied my uncle, whose olive complexion had turned a shade of red. His thick brows lowered, and I half expected smoke to come out of his ears. I hadn't heard of thralls in the two years I'd lived in Dowler, but I'd sensed the undercurrent of a dark secret.

Aunt Matzie stood stiffly. The only other glimpse of her discomfort were her lips parting slightly before she pressed them together again.

"Their lives don't belong to you," the Piper continued. A feral growl added a roughness to his menacing voice. "You will set them free. Or pay the consequences. As for Tanith, I've thought of a fair punishment."

My chest went tight, and I shook my head as the Piper drew me in closer. His hand dropped from my elbow to my waist, yanking me against his hard body so quickly I had to lean on him for support. I could only imagine what everyone else was thinking. They saw me appear with a pointy-eared man in the middle of the night, a man who pulled me close as if midnight trysts were common.

"As the treaty states, anyone or anything who enters my lair is mine. So call your priest or whoever you use to perform ceremonies. As punishment, Tanith shall marry me."

My mouth fell open, and suddenly it was hard to breathe. The pain in my chest increased and I swayed, dizzy. This could not be happening. He hadn't just said *marriage*? Had he?

I'd been engaged before I'd left Solynn, but I had received no letters from my betrothed, George, in a year, adding to my desire to return to the city. He'd promised to write and find a place for us to live, especially because my aunt and uncle had persuaded me to grieve in Dowler and return to Solynn when I was ready. I'd broached the subject recently since they had taken control of my dowery and inheritance. It had only led to an argument with my uncle, and the realization that if I wanted to leave, I had to take control of my future.

Now, I glanced at my aunt and uncle, silently pleading for help. Lord Faren would never agree to it. There had to be a way out. But my uncle waved his hand. "Bring the priest."

5. Tanith

"I'm not marrying you," I whispered as the hall buzzed with hushed voices.

The priest plodded in, his considerable girth bouncing as he moved, the remnants of his thinning hair sticking straight up as he caught his breath. He was dressed immaculately, as though he'd already been up, and even carried the golden rod which was always by his side.

I'd never liked the priest, and I liked him even less now that he was forcing me to make a vow I was in no way ready to make.

The Piper's fingers dug into my side as he bent his head to my ear. "If you don't marry me, your punishment will be much worse. Is that what you want?"

"If you force me to marry you, you'll be sorry."

"Quite the contrary, I hear marriage is delightful."

"One doesn't punish someone by marrying them," I snapped, irritated by his gall.

"I think it's a fitting punishment, considering how upset you are, but after the wedding, I propose to make you a deal."

"You didn't think to propose marriage, but you'll propose a deal?"

"Patience, my love, details later. Just know it will annul the marriage should you choose to comply."

The fight went out of me at those curious words. He'd force me to marry him and then allow me an out? I'd take the deal no matter what, although my mind swam with thoughts. Was it wise to trust the word of the Devil of Dowler? I'd need to make my own plan if I wished to secure my freedom from him. I'd learned to sneak in and out of the impenetrable palace. How hard could it be to escape from the Piper? There was still the issue of money to secure passage back to Solynn, but I was resourceful. I'd figure something out.

The priest cleared his throat while my uncle whispered to him. I squirmed as the Piper released my waist, tucking my hand under his arm again.

"Enough with the theatrics. I'm in a bit of a hurry. Speak the vows, Priest, so that I might take my new bride home. She's had a long night and you choose to make it longer still."

"A few items first." My uncle cleared his throat. "You will be allowed to marry my niece if you agree to the following—"

"I will agree to nothing," the Piper interrupted darkly. "I made my demands, and if you refuse to meet them, what happened in the past will become the present."

I expected more from my uncle, but he blanched visibly and waved his hand. "Proceed with the marriage."

The murmur of voices grew louder, as though the lords and ladies, servants, and guards couldn't quite believe what was happening. I couldn't either, but I could see no way out, and despite the tremor in my body, it was easier to face the Piper than my uncle's anger.

Powerless to stop the marriage, I stilled as the priest stepped forward and spoke. It felt as though I were outside of my body, a mere spectator, watching the proceedings as horror twisted in my gut. The betrayal from my uncle stung, but it was not a shock considering how I'd been treated since I arrived. My aunt was too meek to speak out against her husband, and her silence was more infuriating than anything else. If my mother and father were still alive, they'd never let anything like this happen to me.

A shadow moved at the end of the hall, and Carter's wide-eyed stare captured mine. Relief sang through me. Carter and his brother wouldn't suffer for my mistakes. I gave the slightest shake of my head and he disappeared.

Words gathered like dust in my throat as the priest prompted me. "Tanith, do you promise to love and obey your husband to the end of days?"

Obey. That hated word. "I do," I said, even though I didn't. Words were simply words, right? There would be no harm in breaking a vow.

At the very end, when the priest intoned, "You may seal this wedding by kissing the bride," the Piper turned to me.

Smoothly, he glided one hand through my curls, drawing my face toward his. My heart kicked, and a roaring began in my ears, so loud it almost drowned out his words.

"Let me kiss you," he demanded, smirking.

Before I could say yes or no, his lips were on mine. They were soft and my pulse throbbed. A sudden warmth flooded my lower body, and instinctively, I leaned into him. His fingers tightened in my hair, his mouth possessed mine, stopping just shy of stroking his tongue into my mouth. Everything within me said yes, but the rational side of my brain screamed no. This was the Devil of Dowler. I shouldn't enjoy his sinful kiss.

He pulled away as if he knew what I was thinking and turned his attention back to the hall.

"Now for the magic-thralls," he announced, letting go of me completely.

I gasped for air to calm my racing heart, my mind still a whirl from that brief yet delicious kiss. In the spirit of defiance, I glared at him and wiped my lips with the back of my hand. I tried not to consider what would happen when we returned to his castle. Would he kiss me again? Longer? And why did my legs feel weak from his touch?

Lord Faren's stern tone drove away those thoughts as he announced, "There are no magic-thralls, and even if they were, we would not free them. You've made your demands, now go."

The Piper's face hardened, and if I'd thought he was dangerously handsome before, my mind changed as fury seethed around him. Folding his arms over his chest, he said, "You've made your choice then. I'll give you once last chance to reconsider."

"No," Lord Faren said with kingly authority in his baritone voice. "Now take your bride and leave."

"Wait," Aunt Matzie protested. "Let her have her

things." She moved toward me, holding a satchel she must have sent Uropa to pack. It was heavier than I expected, but as my fingers closed around the handle, my aunt squeezed my arm. Was she trying to tell me something?

Just as quickly, she slipped away while the Piper stared at my uncle. "Your choice has sealed your doom."

Quick as a flash, he pulled out a flute, a long, thin reed of an instrument. The brown wood was carved with golden symbols that swirled and glowed. Without ceremony, he lifted it to his lips and played.

The entire court stood frozen, staring at the Piper's underwhelming retaliation. For some reason, I'd expected him to pull out a weapon, not a flute. Then I remembered. He was the Piper. Of course he played the flute, for it *was* his weapon. Dread coursed through me.

Faintly, I heard my uncle giving orders. "Guards, seize him!"

But the music flared out like a spell, a dance of notes tripping over each other like dancers gaining their balance after a lengthy time without practice. The notes intertwined, then surged across the hall like a wave, bouncing off the columns before sinking into the stone. A rush came, like the sound of many wings from afar, and the doors to the courtyard opened with a boom.

I jumped, spinning to face the blackness of the night as guards rushed the Piper. This would be over in a moment. They'd throw him in prison, and I'd have to face Lord Faren's fury.

But the guards stopped just short of reaching him, as if repelled by some invisible force. They swung their swords to fight their way through, and the air was filled with high-pitched chirps and shadows.

6. Tanith

The cloud of shadows soared into the hall, accompanied by a high-pitched chirping that made my skin crawl. I ducked, pressing my hands to my ears to keep from hearing that awful sound, but it was impossible to keep it out. Wings fluttered. Something velvet touched my cheek. I pressed my lips together, squeezed my eyes shut and waiting for it to go away. But it didn't.

Screams of terror echoed through the palace along with the sounds of running, glass shattering, and then my uncle bellowing, "Call the sorcerers!"

Sorcery. Suddenly the air was foul, an octane of bitter evil pulsing in the updraft of the creatures in flight. I peeked an eye open, then slowly rose, mouth open.

A halo of golden light surrounded the Piper and

me, a barrier that protected us from the circle of guards hemming us in. Someone had roused the archers, and they stood at the end of the hall, shooting arrows at the cloud of darkness while the lords and ladies and servants fled. The chipping buzzed louder in my head, but when I took my hands away from my ears, the lure of the flute drowned out the noise.

The creatures swooped down, dividing into smaller groups before surging through open doors and down passageways, high wails of terror following in their wake. I watched them weave and soar with wings that fluttered too quickly, pointed ears, smashed in faces, and beady black eyes on either side of their tiny heads. Bats. The Piper had called an army of bats to terrorize the palace. Clever.

When I looked at him, it was hard to believe he was the same Piper who'd kissed me, making my skin tingle from head to toe. Although his lips were pursed around the flute and his fingers danced skillfully up and down the body of his instrument, his eyes were marbles of fury. He tilted his head to the left, and the bats soared in that direction. When he moved to the right, they followed, his song controlling them. When he took a step back, I froze. But as he took another step back and another, I followed, clutching the satchel.

The guards stumbled out of the way, still unable to penetrate the barrier that surrounded us. When we reached the entrance, silver moonlight shone down on that demon horse, its bone-white wings spread, waiting for us.

The Piper took the flute from his mouth, even as the last strains of his music still hovered. When he spoke, he directed his words toward my uncle, who stood in the middle of his chaotic court surrounded by guards. "Lord Faren, let it be known that your stubborn heart has brought misery, not only to your household, but to all the people of Dowler. I shall return to give you another chance, but I warn you, if you do not free the magic-thralls, the next scourge will be worse."

"Sorcerers!" roared Lord Faren.

My skin crawled as men in white robes swept into the room. Each one held a golden rod, just like the priest. When they began to chant, the Piper leaped into the horse and pulled me up in front of him. Holding me tight, he urged the horse away from the palace.

The ride back to the Piper's lair was more frightening than the one to the palace, and a sinking sensation washed over me. Too much had happened in one night, leaving me numb and weary. A slew of questions filled my mind, popping up like mushrooms in the forest. I wanted to confront the Piper, but the soullessness I'd seen in his eyes bothered me. His temper might be like my uncle's. I didn't want to broach a hostile conversation while he was still angry.

Darkness greeted us when we arrived back at his castle, the towers looming over us, sharp-edged and glinting like monstrous fangs. He wasted no time in leaping down from the horse. When I tried to jump down by myself, he reached for me. I expected his grip to be tight, bruising, but his hands on my waist were gentle. Once again, he tucked my hand under his arm and escorted me, quickly and wordlessly, through the castle.

As before, the lights lit up when we appeared and faded once we'd passed. Words lay trapped in my throat as the realization sunk in. This was my home now and the Devil of Dowler was my husband. Fitting punishment for my crime of theft? At least in my uncle's eyes. He hadn't even attempted to stop the wedding. It was clear the magic-thralls, whatever they were, were more important to him.

We reached a room and I got the sense it was big and airy, but this time, no mysterious candles lit themselves. Instead, the Piper opened a door and pushed me inside. "Rest," he said curtly, slamming the door behind him.

Throat dry, I spun around, but darkness met me at every corner, making it impossible to see. At last, the antics of the night caught up with me, and I sank to my knees, leaning heavily against the door. What was I going to do?

I opened my eyes, refusing to be overcome by my situation, even though my eyelids were heavy and I could think of nothing better than lying down and going to sleep. But it was dark, and rather unkind of the Piper to toss me in a pitch black room and leave me alone. I tossed away the other alternative, that he could have put me in his room and made me sleep in his bed. My lower belly clenched at the idea of sharing a bed with him. But he'd also promised to annul the marriage, should I comply with his demands. I wanted to hear his proposal, but I was grateful he'd left me alone.

"I need a light," I whispered to the blackness, searching the pockets of my cloak.

The Piper had done his work well, for even my candle and flint were gone, and I doubted my aunt would have had more packed in the satchel. She'd sent Uropa away instantly. As if she'd known. An icy shiver went through me as something bumped against the carpeted floor.

The sound came from inside the room, and my fingers twitched, tempted to reach for the door handle, but I assumed the Piper had locked me inside. I stayed my hand, for knowing I was trapped was worse than facing what was inside.

Panic clawed up my throat as the thump came again, followed by a hiss. A tiny ball of fire no larger than my fist, bloomed, then faded, followed by a belch.

Tiny flames licked at the hearth of a fireplace, slowly growing as they lapped at the wood, like a kitten lapping at a bowl of milk. The castle was enchanted.

Pressing a hand to my heart, I leaned forward and squinted at the shape in front of the fire. It was the size of a cat, gray like stone, with enormous eyes, reptilian nostrils, and a forked tongue that licked its snout as it gazed at me. Four legs, two horns, bat-like wings, and a snout. It patiently returned my stare, its face made less ugly by those overly large, round eyes. I detected no malice, but it looked just like a stone statue until it blinked. I snapped my fingers. It was a gargoyle! This nightmarish night was full of surprises, but this one wasn't so terrible.

"Did you light a fire because I asked?"

The gargoyle moved its head up and down, then crouched on all fours, waving its serpentine tail. Despite everything disastrous that had happened tonight, I smiled. It was ugly but cute, a little pet in my room.

I stood, taking in my surroundings as the light from the fire grew stronger. It was a simple room with a large bed covered in black blankets and lacy drapery. Against one wall was a wardrobe and a vanity with a mirror. A chaise lounge perched beside the fireplace and a plain, high-backed chair sat against the wall. Simple, not cozy or overly lavish, but it would do.

I glanced back at the fireplace, which had elaborate stones with winged statues carved on it. The gargoyle fit in, easy to overlook if I hadn't seen him blink.

"I'll think of a name for you," I promised. "Thank you for the light. I suppose I should unpack."

As soon as the words left my mouth, I realized I'd said it as though I were staying a long time. Giving myself a shake, I put the satchel on the bed and opened it. I'd rest tonight so I'd be ready to spar with the Piper tomorrow. Surely he wouldn't keep me locked in this room. If I gained his trust and showed him I would comply with his demands, he'd let down his guard and I'd flee, stealing some of the valuables in the castle to finance my escape. I just needed to be patient and smart, and wait for an opportunity to present itself.

Inside the satchel were clothes, and the first item I touched was my nightgown. I frowned. How had Uropa known to pack my nightgown? I also pulled out four dresses, one pair of trousers, a loose-fitting shirt, and then gaped in mild astonishment at the two items that lay in the bottom. The first I picked up with trembling fingers as a surge of gratefulness rushed over me. It was a short knife, a dagger really, sheathed in leather with a belt that would be easy to tie around my waist or leg. Aunt Matzie had been watching out for me. How did she know?

The second item was a leather-bound journal tied shut with a string. Even in the light from the fire, I detected the pyramid symbol on the front. I ran my fingers over it, tracing the raised design. Reverently, careful not to tear the fragile pages, I flipped it open. Scrawled in messy handwriting was a ditty I'd heard before:

Beware the Pied Piper
His song sweet yet sinister
Hellbent on revenge
His people to avenge
Beware your last breath
For his flute sings death

A warning. I frowned and as I turned the page, a

letter fell out. Tucking the book under my arm, I unfolded the sheet, greeted by the familiar sight of Aunt Matzie's handwriting.

If you are reading this, he has returned. He goes by many names: Piper. Devil of Dowler. His legendary power contained in a magical flute. Tales have spread about him, forming into legends, outlandish and buried in myth, but within these pages, you'll find a collection of truths gathered from the ancient books of knowledge. I've put this together in hopes that whoever finds this might read it, discover his weakness, and find a way to save us.

7. Tanith

In the beginning, the Creator designed the celestial and the mundane…

Those were the first words of the book, and I continued to read, drawn into an account of the creation of the world and the gifting of talents to the four divines. At its very core, creation involved the vibration of sound, what we called music. Each divine used a relic to carry sound for them, a sort of buffer against the extraordinary power of raw magic. As time passed, people lost their faith in the Creator and the divines. They followed their own way, forgetting about magic and power, and soon those unique abilities became rare and coveted. But there were those who did not forget. They sought those with magic, rounded them up, and kept them as slaves to grow cities and empires and demolish their enemies.

AT SOME POINT I must have fallen asleep, for a light woke me. I was still in my dress and dusty cloak, sprawled across the bed. My thick, black curls cushioned my head, and when I opened my eyes, blinking blearily, lazy, amber eyes gazed back at me. A shudder went down my spine, making me tremble from head to foot. I'd forgotten about my delicious, albeit dangerous, husband.

He leaned against the doorframe, making no move to come in further. I detected no malice in his gaze, but that meant nothing. He kept his expression blank, his assessing gaze roving over me. I studied him back, taking in the fall of his fox-red hair, smooth and straight, yet his ears still stuck out, reminding me he wasn't human. His shirt was clean, white with ruffled sleeves and a plunging v that displayed his smooth chest. It must be his style, I decided, but his trousers fit today, clinging to his slim body. My face went warm when I saw his bare feet, a reminder that I was in his home.

"Join me for breakfast on the patio," he invited, lips curling as if in jest.

With that, he slipped away, the edge of his shadow fading into the adjoining room. Heart pounding, I snatched up the journal, which lay by my hand. Had he seen it? How careless I'd been to fall asleep without hiding the book. What if he'd grown curious, picked it up, and my aunt's note had fallen out? Now I understood her actions. She'd seen me enter, must have recognized the Piper—although I could not imagine how she knew who he was—and guessed he'd take me as a hostage.

Stumbling out of bed, I tossed off the cloak, my eyes skating across the room for a place to hide the book. At last, I tucked it under one of the pillows. It was a pathetic hiding place, but I wasn't sure what else to do, and my dress had no pockets. It would be odd to wear my cloak again, and the Piper had already searched it once. He'd likely do so again if inspired.

Leaving my untamable curls wild, I made my way to the vanity, which held a basin of water, a washcloth, and a towel. I freshened up as much as I dared, unwilling to strip when the door stood open, but the Piper did not return.

I put on a blue dress, hopelessly wrinkled since I'd left the clothes folded at the foot of the bed. A morning without a maid was odd, but I'd get used to it. With another peek at the door, to ensure he wasn't watching, I reached for the dagger and held it up. Fitting it around my waist would be asking for the Piper to take it, but hiding it under my clothes meant access would not be easy. Still, carrying the dagger was better than not having it. At last, I settled on my thigh, tying it so the dagger was on the outside. I'd have to hitch my skirts almost to my waist to get it, but at least I had a weapon.

My room appeared gloomier in daylight—a lair of mystery—and I glanced at the embers glowing in the fireplace. Had there truly been a gargoyle last night? He appeared like a statue now, eyes closed in stone. With a shrug, I took a deep breath and walked out of the room to confront the Piper.

As I'd guessed, his bedroom adjoined mine. His bed, despite being much bigger than mine, was swallowed by the massive room, with its accents of crimson velvet, white lace, and a chandelier hanging from the ceiling. There was a desk covered in books and scrolls, chairs by the fire, a couch in front of the bed, and a bookshelf with an odd assortment of trinkets on it.

Floor to ceiling windows took up one wall, most of them covered with crimson curtains. The door to the balcony stood open, and golden sunlight lured me out, a cloudless day with a gentle breeze.

The Piper sat in a chair, sipping tea and appearing far more elegant than I would have assumed possible. I sat down across from him, stomach rumbling as I eyed the generous spread. This was richer than my uncle's palace, and a wry grin covered my face. "Do you cook?" I asked, determined to get along with him.

His mouth twitched as if he were trying to hold back a laugh. "I have servants."

Spreading a cloth napkin in my lap, I picked up my cup, brimming with what smelled like a peppermint brew. "I haven't seen any."

"So last night, the fire lit itself?"

I almost dropped my cup, eyes widening. "The gargoyle?"

"Ask and he will do his best to please you," the Piper said matter-of-factly, as if everyone had gargoyles for servants.

"Oh." I lost my breath for a moment. "Does he talk? Have a name?"

"My servants are mute. After all, they are made of stone." He chuckled, then leaned across the table to fill his plate. "Help yourself."

I stared at him, rendered mute with surprise. There was something less devilish and more chivalrous about him in the daylight. Emboldened, I reached for a cinnamon cake and regarded him.

Before I lost my courage, I plunged into my next question. "You call yourself the Piper, but do you have a name?"

Picking up a sausage, he chewed it slowly, considering.

I froze, unable to eat as I waited for him to decide. His name must hold more weight than I realized, yet I'd given him mine without a thought.

"After all, why not," he said to himself. "You are my wife."

As if I could forget our midnight wedding, the bats that terrorized the palace, and my uncle calling his sorcerers as we fled.

"My name is Oren."

"Oren," I repeated. It fit him and sounded much less threatening than the ominous, vague title of "the Piper."

Allowing myself a minor victory in winning his name, I bit into the pastry and cinnamon danced across my tongue.

We ate in silence for a few moments, and I chased away thoughts of the future while I ate pastries and sausage, a sharp cheese, tiny green grapes, and a juicy red fruit that looked like blood as it dripped down my chin. Once full, I felt armed for my conversation with Oren.

Guessing my thoughts, he smirked as he poured another steaming cup of tea. "Tanith, are you ready to hear my proposal?"

Patting my mouth with a napkin, I straightened up. "Yes."

He bared his teeth, the sunlight highlighting the razor sharpness. Despite my intent to be on my best behavior, I grumbled, "You've already forced me to marry you, you don't have to intimidate me too."

A sly smile gathered at the corners of his mouth. "Are you intimidated? You don't act like it."

My attitude soured, and I glared at him. "I'm more curious about the proposal which will annul our marriage."

He wagged a finger. "Yes, but only if you meet my demands. I've been sleeping for years, but not much has changed in Dowler. You've lived in the fortress of secrets, the palace ruled by your aunt and uncle. I need information, and you're going to provide it. You'll be my spy and find out what I need to know. If you succeed and I get what I want from your uncle, then the vows of our marriage will break, and you can go your own way in peace. However, if you fail, then you and I will be bound together until death rips us apart. So there's your incentive to help me. Tell me, Tanith, what do you think?"

"I'll do it," I agreed quickly, partly because I didn't have another choice and partly because serving as his informant would give me an opportunity to undermine him. My aunt had asked me to destroy him, and with the notes from the journal, I hoped to discover his weakness and use it to undo his magic. Because if he were gone, I'd be free from his heinous plan.

Oren frowned. "You agreed rather quickly. I thought someone like you might think it over or at least try to bargain."

"What is there to think over? You want the magic-thralls and I want to be free of you and Dowler. This plan of yours is mutually beneficial."

He narrowed his eyes and his voice dropped to a purr. "You have a secret, don't you, Tanith? I'm going to find out and then I'll ruin you. They don't call me the Devil of Dowler for nothing."

My heart thumped in my throat, and suddenly the blade tied to my thigh seemed insufficient, considering his threat. Recalling the fable, I dropped my head, sure the fear in my eyes would betray me. When I could breathe evenly again, I lifted my chin. "You don't know me at all, Oren. Just because I agreed to your proposal doesn't mean I have a hidden agenda."

"I know a lie when I hear it," he leaned over the table. "Enjoy your breakfast, Tanith. I'll find you when I have questions."

With those words, he swept away, leaving me to try and calm my racing pulse.

8. Oren

Tanith. What a curious creature. Even though she was human, I liked my new wife. She made herself mine by waking me up, a trick I was still trying to decipher. She had taken the pyramid from my coffin and her blood—I assumed—covered it, but that should not have been enough to wake me. Not unless she held magic. But when I'd kissed her, I hadn't tasted magic. Although I didn't need to marry her, it was easier to protect her with my magic if we had a sacred vow between us. I doubted she meant the words she'd spoken in the palace, but the trick had worked all the same.

Humans could be so flippant with promises and oaths, believing everything could be undone should they change their minds on some random whim. Guided by emotions, they rarely considered the consequences of their actions. In fact, I doubted Tanith was sorry for stealing from me, only remorseful that she'd gotten caught. Instead of dissolving into tears and begging, she was feisty, sharp-tongued, and beautiful—wild curls, dark eyes, full lips. I wanted to hear her gasp when I kissed her, her throaty moans of arousal and the catch in her voice when she begged for more. As she would, in time. I'd suspected her attraction, and when I'd kissed her, the heat between us had ignited.

I tapped a rhythm on my leg as I recalled her attitude at breakfast. Again, no tears, only a determined streak. She presented a challenge, and while I hoped our deal would work, I was under no false pretense. She'd seek escape as soon as possible and appointing her a gargoyle as a guard wouldn't change that. Nor would frightening her into submission.

Eventually, I'd explain more about our situation and the magic-thralls. For now, I did not trust her as far as tomorrow, no matter the budding attraction I held for her. Outside, I strode to the adjoining building and paused before the structure that had once been a barn. I lifted my flute to my lips, closed my eyes, and played.

I had missed this—the smell of sweet grass, the warmth of the sun on my skin, and most of all, my music. A song welled up within me and melodies swirled like stars, colliding and crashing in a beautiful symphony of song. When I played, everything else floated away, my desires morphing into actions as I sent out my summons.

Last night, I'd awakened the gargoyles, and soon the beasts would come. I was grateful my horse hadn't strayed far, but in the past, he'd always come with a whistle. The others were bold and would have explored far and wide. They might return in days or weeks, depending on how far they'd gone.

I played until the breeze carried my song. Leaves rustled like chimes and the mocking birds picked out the notes, sharing it from one to the other, calling, calling. I stopped to listen and the echoes of my song carried. Enough for today.

My castle perched on a hilltop, the area surrounded by woods and thickets, but down a path, a river warbled. It just so happened the river flowed down to Dowler and surrounded the town. In the past, it had been the source of life, where the inhabitants went to fish and collect water for their daily use. Water. The source of life.

A wicked idea sprang to mind, and I rubbed my hands together with glee. I needed to send a message to Lord Faren. Once I'd spirited Tanith away last night, his sorcerers had likely used their magic to chase away the bats. The message was obvious.

Those in the palace would suffer for the sins of Lord Faren and his ancestors. But I needed a bigger message, a bolder one, to let Lord Faren know his actions would affect the entire city. The river would provide a way.

Kneeling by the bank, I dipped a finger in the water and tasted it. Clean. Sweet. The castle had sufficient water, and when I fished, I fished for pleasure, not need. We would be fine without the resources from the river. Pulling my knife from my belt, I held my hand out, palm up, and slowly sliced the skin open. I pressed my lips together against the pain before plunging my hand into the water.

Blood floated around my arm, a dark melody of crimson slowly spreading to the surface. Blood. Life. Energy. I watched it float, my eyes narrowing as I recalled a rumor about me. Legend held that I drank the blood of children to give me everlasting life. I'd done nothing to combat those rumors, finding them absurd. Children were too young to have blood worth drinking, not to mention the blood of an adult was more potent. Blood gave me power over others, but this time, it had been Tanith's blood that had awoken me. If I tasted it, I'd find out why, but now was not the time to focus on that dark thought.

Dropping the knife, I put my flute to my mouth and played a short, awkward tune with one hand. I needed the magic to work, not necessarily for the notes to be perfect.

The cool waters numbed the pain of my self-inflicted injury, and slowly, the blood flowed faster, a stain covering the surface of the water. It drained out of me, slowly but surely, and weakness consumed me. I sank further to the ground, unable to play, holding the flute in one hand. This was drastic magic, dangerous, but I'd come back from the dead to win, and this time, I'd go to any extreme to free the thralls.

9. Tanith

Questions burned inside me once Oren left and I waited, breathless, but silence came from within. Oren. I liked his name for it almost made him sound mortal, human. I was deeply curious about him and his plans, but I had to make my own.

When I entered the bedroom, the door to the hallway was open. My heart leaped. I wouldn't be trapped like a prisoner in the bedrooms. But where to explore? And would I find my way back if I left the room? Aunt Matzie wanted me to find Oren's weakness, and I wanted to return to Solynn. Money was my only hinderance, but Oren was sly. To outwit him, I had to take a chance that he hadn't counted on my boldness.

Returning to the room I'd slept in, I put on my

cloak, shaking as much dust out of it as possible. The gargoyle by the fireplace looked so much like a statue. If not for Oren's words, I would have assumed last night was just my imagination. Pulling out the journal and my aunt's letter, I stood in front of the mantel and announced, "I need a light."

The transformation was instant. The gargoyle's eyes popped open, and it wagged its tail as though it were absolutely thrilled to serve me. Despite my dire predicament, I laughed as it belched out a ball of fire. Tiny flames licked at the wood, but it was enough. I held the end of the letter in the flame, watching it turn to black ash.

"Thank you," I told the gargoyle. "You're adorable, you know, and I still haven't thought of a name for you. I'm going to explore the castle. Would you like to come along?"

He wagged his tail again and inclined his horned head, as if he wanted me to pet him. Dropping the end of the burnt letter, I scratched his head, my fingers pausing as I touched cold stone. My brow furrowed as I stared at the lively eyes and wagging tail. What was this thing? Some odd cross between a cat, a goat, a lizard, and a bird?

"I'm going to call you Pip," I decided, patting his head.

Before leaving the room, I tucked the journal in

the wide pocket of my cloak. If I found a quiet spot, I'd read more, although I still feared Oren would sneak up on me. Regardless, I left the room, the thump of Pip's footsteps beside me.

The castle was a confusing lair of traps. Each time I opened a door, a spiraling staircase led up, never down. Some doors opened into cold rooms with covered furniture, a blanket of dust, and layers of cobwebs strewn about. Creepy. With a shudder, I closed those doors and continued on my fruitless quest. The castle seemed determined to guard its secrets. Was this Oren's magic at work? I imagined him laughing at me from somewhere, for how could I escape if I couldn't find the exit?

In one last spark of defiance, I took the stairs leading up, fingers trailing along the ridges of the railing, taking in the carvings of winged beasts and flowers. The lights lit, as though sensing my presence, but the higher I climbed, the more a strangeness came over me, much like in the crypt. Except this time, it felt like a pressure, pushing down on me. My legs felt weighed down, and my head felt like it was clamped in a vise that slowly squeezed.

When I turned around, Pip was not beside me, but further down the stairs, wagging his tail as if begging me to return. Whatever was upstairs did not want to be seen. What if it was some evil that would hurt me? But what if it were a clue to finding out more about the Piper? I paused, coming to a stand still as the pressure increased.

If my aunt's words were true, I had all the clues in my pocket. I just needed to read the book. With a frown, I addressed Pip. "This has been a fruitless search. I'd like to go back now."

Pip thumped down the stairs. He was quick for a stone beast and proudly led the way back to the bedrooms.

The open doors and sunshine streaming in from the balcony were a welcome relief, and after a quick search, I satisfied myself that Oren had not returned.

During my absence, someone had cleared away breakfast and replaced it with more covered dishes. I lifted the dome-shaped covers to reveal cucumber sandwiches, stripes of smoked fish over a crusty white bread, stuffed eggs, spiced chicken, and an assortment of fruits and tiny cakes, each one the size of my finger. My mouth watered at the sight and I sat down, expecting Oren to join me for lunch.

He never came.

Deciding he had business, even though I did not know what he did, I ate, washed it down with tea and water, and then settled down to read, listening for signs that someone was coming.

I read about magic and muses, talents and old

trees, and how the magic of the world had become lost as times shifted and changed. The book didn't seem like a collection of knowledge about the Piper, but more of a history of magic. It made no sense to my predicament, and I skipped a few pages impatiently, trying to figure out what Aunt Matzie had wanted the reader to discover.

Taking a break for more tea, I slipped the book in my pocket and leaned out over the balcony. A jolt went through me. Of course. The balcony was my escape. All I needed to do was find some rope. Leaning out over it, I stared down, my heart sinking as I realized I was four or five stories up in the castle. The fall would be deadly, and I doubted I'd find rope that long. Thoughts churning, I looked to Pip for support, but he lay belly up, warming himself in the sun. For all appearances, he'd turned to stone again. This place was odd.

Unlike at the palace, there were no footholds or grips to keep me from falling on the way down. The balcony dropped straight down, and the land swelled then dipped into thick forest. There were no paths, no animals, and another tower blocked my view of what was beyond. I shivered.

Was I alone in an enchanted castle with stone servants? Who else was here with me, and where was Oren? As much as I didn't want to listen to him,

I wanted him to return. Unease settled like a rain cloud on my shoulders, and even the knife tied to my thigh did not make me feel safe. Crossing to the room, I checked the main bedroom door for locks, for I didn't want to be trapped inside. I closed it and opened it again, and the door obeyed. Feeling better, I returned to the balcony to read.

Oren did not return. That evening, I found a tray outside my door filled with delicacies that made my mouth water. I ate heartily and still he did not come. I had Pip light a fire in Oren's room, since it was bigger and more comfortable. Careful to touch nothing, I studied old maps, scrolls, and drawings of what looked like shooting stars falling from the sky.

When I started to nod off, I retired to my room, noting the bed had been made and my clothes hung in the wardrobe. I lay down and slept soundly, my exhaustion at the change of my situation finally catching up with me.

To my disappointment, in the morning, Oren still had not returned. I spent a fruitless day reading, opening the door to find trays of food, but nothing else. By midday, I was bored and angry with him. Where was he? Had he locked me in his castle only to leave and carry on as if I weren't there? I needed to try harder to escape, and not let the castle bully me into staying.

Besides, I'd finished the journal my aunt had given me, and it was useless—just an account of old magic, beliefs, miracles, and people who believed a higher being would save them if only they asked.

Leaving the balcony, I decided to tie bedsheets together and hope they would reach the ground. I was walking toward Oren's bed when the door swung open.

10. Tanith

Oren sagged against the doorframe, his skin unnaturally pale. My gut twisted with fear at his appearance. His fox-red hair was limp and matted to his neck. Thick globs of mud caked the side of his face and smeared the front of his clothing. Gathering his strength, he took a step into the room, his boots squelching with water. Gingerly, he held one hand to his chest, revealing dried blood on his arm.

I swallowed hard. Had my uncle sent an assassin? "Who attacked you?"

"No one," he whispered hoarsely and pointed to the corner of the room.

I blinked until I saw what I'd overlooked before. A door painted the same color as the walls blended in effortlessly. It opened into a washroom and I scowled. For the past two days, I'd been bathing like a pauper when an ornate, claw-footed tub had been on the other side of the wall?

"Draw a bath," he instructed.

I turned on the water, watching the heat rise as it poured into the tub. When I spun around to leave, Oren stood in the doorway, effectively blocking the exit. With some trouble, he tugged the shirt off his head, smearing more mud across his face. I should have glanced away from his impeccable body, his skin glistening with moisture, displaying no scars or blemishes—at least that I could see.

"Sit." He pointed to a stool in a corner.

I'd wanted Oren to return, but not like this. I did not appreciate sitting in the washroom with him. "I'd rather go."

"Stay."

There was no firmness in his command, and given his state, I knew I could push past him and dash out of the room. When his hands went to the waistband of his trousers, I spun around.

"Have you ever seen a man naked?" He asked, a hint of glee in his tone.

"I was giving you privacy," I retorted.

"I didn't ask for it," he quipped.

A moment later, the water splashed and I took it

as my signal to face him. The water hid his lower body, and he leaned back, closing his eyes.

Another retort rose to my lips, but he appeared so peaceful lying like that, vulnerable, wounded, naked. Not devilish at all. My lower belly tingled with that twitch of attraction, and instead of tearing my eyes away from his perfect form, I eyed the curve of his muscles and the slope of his body until my face warmed. I dropped my gaze, but the memory of his kiss came back. I clasped my hands in my lap, as if that could keep me from acting on my thoughts.

"If I weren't so filthy, would you join me in the tub?"

My eyes flashed to his, noting the laugher behind his amber gaze and the lightness in his tone.

"No," I said firmly. "Why do you jest like that? We both know you have no interest in a marriage."

He sat up and reached for the soap as color returned to his face. Suds formed as he slowly scrubbed away the filth. "I have an interest in you, my thief bride."

"I'm not a thief. Well, not normally a thief. I was driven … forget it." I sighed. "What happened to you? Were you attacked?"

"Magic," he said, soaping his hair with both hands. "Tomorrow we will return to the palace to see what they think of what I've done, and to find out if the sorcerers can create a counter curse."

I pointed an accusatory finger at him. "You did that to yourself for a curse? I thought you'd been attacked or my uncle had sent an assassin!"

"You seem upset, as if you worried about me while I was gone."

His words struck a nerve. "Of course I worried. I was trapped in these rooms and the castle wouldn't let me out. You did that on purpose, didn't you? Making all the doors open to staircases that led up."

To my surprise, Oren's eyes narrowed. "That wasn't my doing, Tanith. The gargoyle is your guard to keep you from escaping. I did not enchant the castle."

"Pip?" I stared.

His brow creased. "Who is Pip?"

"The name I gave to the gargoyle… never mind. If you didn't enchant the castle, who did?"

Instead of answering my question, Oren submerged himself in the water. When he came back up, his hair was slicked down his head and dripped on his broad shoulders. Water droplets clung like dewdrops to his eyelashes, and my stomach twisted at the sight of his full, wet lips and the idea of another heated kiss.

"I don't know, Tanith," he said. "I've been asleep

for a long time and left this castle empty. We might not be the only ones living here."

The idea that we weren't alone sent a chill through me. "What about your servants? You mentioned them?"

"Yes, but none of them have magic that can enchant the castle."

He stood shamelessly, water streaming off him as he stepped out of the tub. I shielded my eyes with my hand. "You could have warned me," I complained.

His dark laugh vibrated through me. "I like to see your reactions. Besides, we're married. There's nothing to hide."

My mouth went dry, but he wasn't propositioning me, not yet at least. I had to be careful before he tricked me out of my clothes.

He toweled off quickly, leaving puddles of water across the stone as he strode into the room. I tried not to look, but couldn't help a glimpse of his bare backside, the muscles of his back, and the dimples just above his bottom. Shifting uneasily on the stool, I was aware of the flush of warmth on my skin, tingling with lust.

I waited a little longer to ensure he'd had time to dress before leaving the washroom. I found him on the balcony, eating the remnants of lunch, licking his fingers after each bite. The politeness of our first breakfast together was lost under his ravenous appetite.

"What are you?" I inquired once he'd finished eating and wiped his hands and mouth on a napkin. "You're not human, not mortal."

His sudden grin made me realize he'd completely recovered from whatever magical ordeal he'd put himself through. "And what will I get for answering your questions?"

"The satisfaction of answering."

A wolfish laugh came out of his mouth and his sharp teeth looked like fangs. "Do you always say unexpected things like this?"

"If you expect me to beg and cry and grovel, that's not who I am. My parents raised me to stand up for myself and to be independent. You are trying to take both those things away by making me your wife and forcing me to serve your interests." I fisted my hands to keep from slapping them over my mouth at that bold statement, but I wouldn't take back my sharp words. He'd abandoned me for a day and a half, and I was no closer to figuring out who he was, nor how to get back to Solynn.

He stepped closer, smelling of pine with faint hints of cinnamon and cloves. Spicy. Dangerous. Tantalizing. My insides fluttered as he took my fist, fingers brushing over the delicate skin of my wrist. Slowly, he undid the bandage around my hand, and my pulse throbbed in response to his touch. I instinctively shifted closer, tilting my head to glare up at him, aware of my hair falling down my shoulders, leaving my neck bare. I thought of his lips, his teeth against my throat, and a surge of feelings betrayed my desire to escape.

"We all pay the price for our mistakes. I'm one of the Fallen, one of the Others, and you're right to believe I'm not human. Otherwise, you could not have woken me up. I'm inhuman."

I struggled to tug my hand away, but his grip tightened.

"What does inhuman mean?" I demanded.

"I can't die, if that's what you're asking. At least, no one has found a way to kill me."

"But how long were you asleep in the crypt?"

"In my coffin? I don't know, fifty years, a hundred years? I haven't taken the time to calculate it. It didn't seem important."

"Then why did you attack the palace? The people who put you to sleep are long dead."

His jaw tightened. "I haven't forgotten what they did to me. That alone I could forgive, but not what your uncle and his sorcerers do. One thing you must learn, Tanith, is that, given the opportunity to change, most people would rather keep things as they are, keep the status quo. Because change is frightening, it tears down all defenses and forces one to begin anew, to rebuild, and that takes work. No one wants to do the work or deal with the repercussions of their actions and deeds, just as you're angry with me for punishing you for your crime."

I jerked away from his grasp. "It's not the same."

"No? How is it different?"

My ears burned. "You're comparing me to my uncle, to things that happened to you a lifetime ago. But you're looking at everything the wrong way, from your own perspective. Do you ever consider anyone else's perspective? The night you set bats loose in the palace, women and children and servants were terrified. Did you think about how your actions might affect them? And there was a reason I was in the crypt. You didn't ask, didn't consider how unhappy this city makes me, how desperate I must have been to escape that I would have done anything, even commit a crime."

My voice rose with each word, bringing me close to tears, even though I hadn't cried since my parents died. Blinking, I stared past him, scowling at the lush scenery as I hugged my arms around my waist.

"No," he admitted at last. "I did not consider each person's personal demons, but I am aware of the impact I have, the fear my name instills. And I will take my fury out on those who do wrong. You'd be wise to remember that, for it was your ignorance that led you astray. If you'd known the legend that haunts this city, you'd understand the crypt is sacred, off limits for a reason. When you stepped inside, you disturbed a magical barrier. You keep blaming me, but you did this. When you woke me up, you made yourself mine."

I flinched, wanting to stalk away, but there was nowhere to go. Besides, it was rather childish to run away in the middle of a disagreement. A laughable thought came to mind. I was having a spat with the Devil of Dowler, and aside from his blazing eyes, he hadn't lifted a finger to harm me. If it had been my uncle, I'd be holding my cheek, waiting for the pain from a slap to subside. "You understand magic. Why don't you change the rules?"

"I use magic, but I can't change the rules," he snorted. "I can't change something that exists beyond the foundation of the world."

Impatiently, I tapped my foot against the stone. "What about your flute?"

"It is the conductor for my power."

He was so open about it and my thoughts went back to the journal. Maybe it wasn't useless. I simply had to find out more about the Piper and how magic worked. He couldn't be killed, but he could be weakened or put back to sleep. Surely my uncle with his sorcerers could make that happen. Then, I'd be free of him, but right back where I started under the rule of my uncle, unless I figured out how to escape from him too.

"May I see it?" I asked tentatively.

His eyes flashed, and he stepped back, as if I'd asked him something intrusive and personal. "No," he said briskly. "Enough of this. We have work to do."

Striding back into the room, he tugged on his boots and started for the door. "Aren't you coming?"

Of course he'd said "we."

I followed. "Are you going to find out what else might lurk in the castle?"

"Another time. Our business is urgent."

Curious, I followed him out of the room.

11. TANITH

The castle opened for us, bright and airy, stairs leading down instead of up, spaces still covered with dust. Oren strode with purpose, not looking to see if I followed. I paid close attention to the path we took, right out of the bedroom, down a wide flight of stairs, through another set of halls, down again, and yet again.

The main level was filthy and smelled of mold and rot. Heavy, black curtains covered the windows, blocking any traces of light as though the castle were a tomb, hiding secrets in the shadows.

Heavily decorated doors led outside, and although I'd been on the balcony, it was quite different to feel the grass beneath my feet again. I took a deep breath of the sweet summer air, tasting freedom. Thick woods rose on all sides, pine trees waving in the breeze, sending the spicy scent to my nose. The one benefit to living in Dowler versus Solynn was the wildness of the scenery and the closeness to nature. If the rules of the palace weren't so strict, and if I hadn't been grieving for my parents, I might have wanted to stay.

But the moment I set foot in Dowler, a sourness had tainted my sojourn and now this. Married to an inhuman and surrounded by magic. It was so horrible, I could have laughed. Back in the city, things like this did not happen.

"The woods are treacherous, in case you're thinking of running." Oren casually tossed the words over his shoulder.

"I wasn't," I lied and then added, "How come the castle opened for you?"

"Lesser magic doesn't work on me. I suspect whoever is inside doesn't want to test me. Did you notice anything unusual while I was... gone?"

"Everything is unusual," I quipped. "But there was a pressure when I started going up, as if the castle didn't want me to. And Pip wouldn't come."

"Hmm." Oren grunted. "One problem at a time."

An unwelcome house guest sounded like more than a problem, but I shrugged it off as we entered another building, a barn with swinging doors and rows of stalls. The itchy scent of hay made me want to sneeze, even though here, unlike the castle, it was clean. "Is this where you spent your time?" I asked, grumbling.

"I had the servants clean the barn first, for my familiars to return."

The way he said familiars made me think of witches, known for having an odd alliance with wild beasts. Witches could read minds, share thoughts, and sometimes shape shift. Despite those being mere stories, in Oren's presence, I knew there was a glimmer of truth to every old tale.

"What are your familiars?"

"Beasts of the forest, usually. It depends on who heard my call and returned."

As he spoke, a black and white cat poked its head out of a stall and twirled around Oren's legs, purring. He stroked its head before continuing toward the back of the stable. I glimpsed two pure white owls sitting in the rafters, asleep, as the cat disappeared back into the hay. A donkey stood in one stall, chewing and staring back at me with bored eyes. But I did not see the death horse from the night of my wedding.

Oren strode ahead while I meandered, studying the barn—the tack hanging from the wall, a ladder leading up a loft, a wheelbarrow, shovel and other gardening tools in a corner. Oren threw open double doors to reveal a workshop. I paused at the entrance, eyes widening as he revealed yet another secret.

The workshop had a table, shelves lined with cloth, and statues wearing bright clothing. It reminded me of a tailor's shop. Perhaps Oren wasn't just a piper bent on revenge. There was more to him, wasn't there? Just as there was more to me. I wasn't simply an unhappy orphan, grieving the loss of my parents and frustrated with my bad luck. I wished to be the woman I had been before my parents' tragic death, my dreams for the future bright and unspoiled.

"You were a tailor in a past life," I said, hoping to draw more out of Oren.

"A tailor?" He turned the word over, as if he'd never heard it, then followed my gaze to the table and chuckled. "No, I was trained as a healer and my steady hands make it easy to make clothes."

His past was a surprise to me, for it was the opposite of what he was doing now: spreading chaos and fear wherever he went. "A healer? Do you still practice the art?"

"No, I rarely get visitors up here, in the past the forest creatures used to come by so I could tend to their wounds."

I narrowed my eyes as I reconsidered the tales spread about the Piper. Why couldn't he just be harsh and evil? It would be much easier to flee if I didn't know his heart was tender enough to care for the animals in the wood, to bind their wounds and give them shelter. That side of him differed from the furious man who'd plagued the palace with bats.

I didn't like the thoughts my mind entertained. Maybe he wasn't so bad. I'd heard of arranged marriages where the couple got used to each other and eventually fell in love. A new plan struck me at the thought. I'd harden my heart against him, but if I could make him fall in love with me, maybe he'd let me walk away instead of using me for his plans.

"You appear thoughtful," Oren said, spreading his materials out on the worktable. "Come, I need your opinion."

His words would be my undoing if I wasn't careful. Putting the table between us, I stared down at the dark-colored material. "What is this for?"

"You, my little thief, need to blend in when you're sneaking through the palace. I'm guessing the bag your aunt packed was full of dresses, but nothing that would allow you to stalk about unseen."

Ah. He had noticed that exchange. I was glad I'd burned the letter. "Err ... no."

"Then I will make you a proper outfit, but first, tell me all you know about the vaults in the palace."

I chewed on my lower lip. "What vaults?"

Tapping his fingers impatiently on the table, he explained. “They are underneath the palace, often guarded. I imagine few are allowed beneath the lower level, which connects to the temple where the priests mask the magic of the sorcerer.”

My mind spun at the idea. I’d guessed something nefarious was going on in the palace, something I wasn’t privy to, but this was unimaginable. Words tumbled out of my mouth in haste, my discomfort giving way to babbling. “There’s a curfew every night. No one may walk the streets, and if caught, they must endure a public whipping. The palace is similar. After midnight, everyone is restricted to their rooms except for the guards and specific servants, but I’ve never known why. The palace has harsh rules. Walking alone is frowned upon, and exploring is forbidden. Once I found these locked doors, and I guessed they might lead to a lower level. My uncle was furious when he found me, he hit me, and … well, it made me wonder what was behind those doors.”

Oren’s expression darkened. “Did he hit you often?”

That was what he picked up on? “Yes … er … no, only when he was angry. I … I did not grow up here and getting used to the rules has been a difficult adjustment.”

"And your aunt, did she ever allude to the use of magic?"

"She's a very quiet woman and keeps her thoughts to herself. She's not unfriendly, but she's not … warm. Besides, her children—my cousins—take up most of her time." It felt good to share my stressors with Oren and he listened, nodding as if he understood.

"You are going to find out what is behind those doors," he announced.

My heart kicked. "I can't. If my uncle finds me down there again, you don't know what he will do to me. Besides, you're the one with magic. Why can't you play your flute and force the doors open?"

"It's complicated, and I don't have time to explain the logistics of magic to you. If I go gallivanting around the castle, the sorcerers will know. When I perform magic, it leaves a trace, a lingering echo. Besides, they use a dark magic I cannot undo. The doors must open freely, and they must either open from within or with Lord Faren's key."

The thrill of sneaking around the palace was not unlike sneaking into the crypt, and yet my body repelled at the thought of returning there. "I'm not a professional thief, you know," I bristled.

"No, but you have a knack for taking what doesn't belong to you and lying to get yourself out of trouble. But that's not the only reason. You've lived in the palace. You know the ins and outs of it, and that knowledge is much more than I have. Even if you gave me a map, I would not instinctively know what you do. Besides, I have magic which I will use as a decoy. While your uncle and the sorcerers are trying to undo my spells, you will be free to sneak into the vault."

My chest squeezed. I didn't like it, nor did I have a choice. "Why? What is so important that you need my help?"

He ceased what he was doing with the material and leaned over the table, staring directly into my eyes. "What was so important that you ignored all propriety and entered the crypt? I'll answer your question when you answer mine."

"I told you already, I'm leaving Dowler. I only stole to finance my escape."

"Reasons go much deeper than that. There's a turning point for every action, especially when we believe our need to be so great that we ignore every law, every rule set in place, believing we are the exception. But we're not. And then we have to deal with our actions and the consequences left behind."

"Is that what you told yourself when you called the bats? Your need was greater than theirs?"

His lips curled. "I know who I am and what I'm

doing. I make no excuses for my behavior."

I swallowed hard as he glided around the table, keeping me pinned with his glare.

"Do you know why I married you?" he asked.

"To punish me."

"No, to protect you," he corrected, moving into my personal space.

My eyes went wide. "Protect me from what?"

"You and I spoke a sacred vow together, a life bond, and that allows me to protect you with my magic. While you're in the palace working for me, my magic will protect you. I'm not sure how much, but there it is. I wouldn't leave my thief completely vulnerable."

"And I suppose you want me to say thank you."

"I don't need your gratitude." His lips twitched as he slipped his hands around my waist, his fingers grazing my hips. "Now, I'm going to take your measurements so I can make you an outfit. You'll need to lose a bit of your skirt."

He gave me a dark grin and started gathering my dress in his fingers, pulling it up.

My mouth went dry, and I both wanted him to continue and didn't.

"Wait." I wrapped my fingers around his wrist and he stopped immediately. "What are you going to do?"

"I thought I was clear. Take your measurements for the outfit. You do know how to sew, don't you? I'll need help with the stitching."

"I can wear my cloak. It should be sufficient," I protested.

The idea of him getting me out of my dress and down to my small clothes made me shiver. I didn't trust myself to be that unclothed in front of him and still resist his dark charms. And I didn't want to think about why I was attracted to him at all.

"It will not be," he disagreed, brushing his fingers down my leg.

Suddenly, Oren paused. I tried to jerk away, but it was already too late. He'd felt the odd shape of the dagger through my skirt, and his mouth hardened into a thin line. Lifting me up, he sat me on the table. "Lean back," he ordered.

My throat went dry, but I had no recourse except to obey. I leaned back on my elbows while he stood between my legs, holding my gaze as he pulled my dress higher, fingers skimming the bare skin of my knees and then my thighs. Instinctively, I opened my legs wider, shameless as that ache and throb began. He pushed the dress halfway up my thighs, but he was more interested in the dagger. Warm fingers closed around my leg, and suddenly, it was difficult to breathe under the heat of his touch.

"You are full of surprises, Tanith. I dearly hope this wasn't intended for me."

I swallowed hard under his scrutiny, my voice weak when I finally spoke. "No, it's for my protection."

I expected him to take it away—scold me, punish me, anything other than what he actually did. "Keep it then, wife of mine. But if you try to use it against me, you'll be very sorry."

Incredulous, I stared at him. How could he make me feel both weak and strong? My eyes lingered on his mouth until I ripped my gaze away. He was my captor, my husband, with magic I could not explain, but I found it impossible to move. I lay there until he lifted me off the table, allowing my skirts to fall back around my ankles as he measured me. The cat wandered in as he finished. I picked it up and sat down, stroking its fur while it purred, the motion and sound calming my racing heart.

Oren cut, measured with the material wrapped around my body, and then we both began to sewing while the cat roamed. I was glad for something to do with my hands, and the silence between Oren and I was mutual, without tension. In fact, the afternoon held a semblance of normality, which was oddly frightening.

12. Tanith

We spent the night in the barn, Oren only leaving to retrieve the evening meal. He was gone for such a short time, I wondered if his butler had brought it to the barn doors, and how Oren communicated with his stone staff. I tried not to think about gargoyles preparing the food I ate, because frankly, it should have been impossible.

The loft was outfitted with hammocks, which were warm and comfortable. We slept on opposite sides of the loft while the gentle sway of the hammock lulled me to sleep. I woke a few times, startled by the howling of wolves, the crying of a creature in pain, and thrashing in the woods. Secretly, I wondered if Oren wanted to spend the night in the barn to make me aware of the dangers of the forest at night.

But I'd already decided how I'd escape. If he trusted me to spy alone in the palace, I could run. All I needed was money. Even though I was curious about the vault and Oren's vendetta, I couldn't let his plan distract me. I had to flee the moment the opportunity presented itself, and I expected it would be soon.

In the morning, Oren was already gone when I woke. Climbing down the ladder, I found him in the workshop, finishing up my outfit.

"Try it on," he said, tossing the trousers across the table to me. When I hesitated, he turned around. "I won't look."

Keeping an eye on him, I tugged on the trousers, which hung low on my hips. Wiggling out of my dress, I quickly pulled on the shirt. It stretched tight across my chest, but I noticed Oren had sewn pockets within. It was more like a tunic, falling to mid-thigh—allowing me to hide the knife underneath it but providing easy access. Oren's idea. He'd also added hidden pockets to hold any information I needed to steal. The clothes molded perfectly to my body, and I strutted around the workshop, mortified at how impressed I was with Oren's skills. Maybe he wasn't so bad after all. An entire outfit in one day was nothing short of miraculous.

"Better." He surveyed me. "We should go."

"Without breakfast?"

His long legs carried him out of the workshop, and I hastened to follow, thinking of cinnamon buns and another conversation on the balcony.

"What you see today will probably make you lose your meal, and I'd rather not have it all over me," he responded.

My gut twisted in knots as he whistled, summoning the death horse. It was just as eerie in the daylight, appearing like some red-eyed monster that belonged in the underworld—skeletal with velvet skin as black as the crypt. My positive thoughts about the comforts of Oren's home faded as he lifted me onto the horse's back and swung up behind. As his powerful thighs squeezed around me, I wished I were behind him so I'd have something to hold on to. When his muscular arm came around my waist, I clutched it, unashamed, as the horse reared back with a hellish scream and dashed through the forest.

The wind stole my breath as we dashed away from the castle, back toward Dowler. Once the horse slowed to a stop, my entire body trembled from the sheer terror of our reckless gallop. Slowly, I unpeeled my fingers from Oren's arm, glad he said nothing about how tightly I had gripped him.

"Where are we?" I asked, taking in my surroundings.

We were on a grassy knoll overlooking the city. The road lay a few feet away, sloping down into the valley and then back up to the palace. It was designed purposefully, so people were forced to look up and see the palace, the temple, and the mountain —a fortress of protection if a time of need ever came again.

The river flowed down from the mountain and forked into smaller bodies of water that threaded through and around the city. I gasped, my hand flying to my mouth. The water was the wrong color. Instead of shimmering like a diamond in the sunlight, it was a dark crimson, an unnatural hue, and on the surface floated what must be dead fish. We were too far away to see clearly yet, but as the direction of the wind turned, I smelled the rot wafting off the water, the stink of death. My stomach turned.

"What did you do?" I whispered.

"I turned the water to blood."

He sounded immensely proud of himself, and in that moment, I understood the weight of his power, and the toll it took from him. The day and a half he'd been gone had been to do this, to pour his magic into the river until the water turned to blood. Bile rose in my throat, but he had been right to deny me breakfast. Nothing came up.

"How could you?" I cried. "This affects more than just the palace. People who did nothing wrong live here. They have nothing to do with your vendetta against my uncle. How could you do such a thing to them? Water is the source of life! If they can't drink or fish, what will they do?"

His arm tightened around me as he leaned forward. "Let's go to the palace and find out if your uncle is more agreeable today."

Rage swirled in the pit of my belly. I wanted to rip myself out of his grip. How could he toy with the lives of others in such a flippant manner? How could he oppress them like this? He really was the Devil of Dowler.

I fumed as we trotted down the hill and through the city. For a place once so lively, now only silence met my ears. People who'd been looking out closed their doors as we passed. They knew the truth, and guilt racked me because I was the one who'd done this. I'd gone to the tomb and awoken the Piper. This was my fault, and I couldn't flee the city with this weighing on my conscience. I had to do everything in my power to work with my aunt and uncle and quell the Piper's wrath.

My determination hardened as we approached the gates, still broken from the horse smashing into the hinges. Someone had finished the task, taking the gates off and leaning them against the stone.

We thundered into the courtyard, where Oren dismounted. When I looked down at his red hair, it was as if he'd transformed. I no longer saw Oren, but the Piper, a shroud of darkness enveloping him. How was I attracted to this man? Nothing but fury surrounded him.

I opened my mouth to condemn him, but then remembered what I'd done in the crypt. Desperation had driven me to make a choice I wasn't proud of, an action that had unintended consequences. If I found out what was driving the Piper to commit such crimes against Dowler, perhaps I could stop him. My chest went tight as I dismounted. But what if Aunt Matzie was right, and he was carrying out his crimes for no good reason at all? I hated to admit it, but the answers to everything lay within that vault.

Oren's fingers closed around my upper arm, pulling me close so he could direct his words to my ear. "We're going in the front door and all eyes will be on me. Sneak away and see what you can find out about the vault. If Lord Faren keeps the key on his person, I will find it. When the wolf howls, it's time to go."

Without giving me a chance to respond, he released me and trotted up the steps, shaking his hair back as he pushed the doors open. All eyes turned toward him, and then the screams began. I didn't blame them after what he'd done with the bats and now with the blood.

I glimpsed my uncle's furious gaze as I crept toward the entrance. Even the guards standing at the hall moved forward as Lord Faren pointed at Oren and bellowed. "Seize him!"

"You don't want to do that," Oren snapped. "It will be much worse if you do. I came to see if you'd changed your mind."

"No," Lord Faren's voice was hard as stone. "There will be no freedom here. Besides, my sorcerers will undo what you have wrought. If you think to take down my city with bullying and intimidation, I warn you, we will come for you …"

The sound of their voices died away as I moved further into the palace, trying to recall how I'd found the vault before. Then I remembered Oren's words about the temple and headed that way. The palace was pungent with fear. Through open doors, I glimpsed people standing on balconies, likely watching the blood-filled river. Occasionally, I heard a low wail. I was almost at the temple when a voice hissed out. "Tanith?"

Carter's round face peeked out from behind a door. I hurried to him, pressing a finger to my lips. "Carter, I can't be seen with you."

"What happened? Are you alright? I'm sorry, we shouldn't have left you in the tomb, but …"

I shook my head as he trailed off. "It was a terrible idea. I shouldn't have asked you to help me. Where is Kinder?"

"He's fine. We both are, but you … you're married to him." Carter's voice cracked at the end, betraying his emotion.

I frowned. "Yes, but Carter, I have little time. I have to stop him."

"He's here? Now? I can help you—"

"No, you can't. My uncle will be ruthless if he finds out." I closed my eyes briefly. I wanted help, but only I had been punished for entering the crypt. If Carter and Kinder were safe, they needed to remain that way. I alone carried the weight of my mistake. I wouldn't be able to bear it if they were beaten for the part they'd played in waking the Piper too. "Just … stay away from me," I told him.

"But Tanith, you can't do this alone."

No, he was right, but … "You cannot get into trouble on my behalf. You have your brother to think about." And then, because his eyes still disagreed, I added. "Besides, I'm married now and nothing you do can change that."

He flinched as though I'd struck his cheek, then retreated, shoulders slumped like a wounded animal. A heaviness slowed my pace as I walked away from him, sure I'd lost a friend.

13. Tanith

Twice a year, the entire city went to the temple for a ritual of prayers and animal sacrifice. The rite did not surprise me, for there were temples and priests in Solynn. But I had been unprepared for the violence with which the priests butchered a goat and carved out its insides while blood poured over the floor. I'd had to close my eyes so I wouldn't vomit. When I had peeked at Lord Faren, he was watching with rapt attention, almost as if he enjoyed the sight of blood. After that, I'd only gone to the temple when forced.

Now, I slipped through the side entrance, connected to the palace by a short hall. Closing the door gently behind me, I peered into gloom. The candles burned low, and an offering smoked on the altar where two priests kneeled, likely praying for deliverance from the Piper. Walking on my tiptoes, I dared not breathe lest the priests look up and see me.

Even though the head priest—and the sorcerers—were with Lord Faren, I feared discovery. It occurred to me as I crept toward the curtain, that although I was aware sorcerers existed, I hadn't seen one until the night of the bats. The night everything went wrong.

I ducked behind the black curtain, expecting more priests, but the space only revealed more candles and four doors. I hesitated. They were all closed and anyone might be behind them. I had to make a guess that wouldn't get me caught. It wouldn't be one of the first two, I decided, for those doors were too close to the outer walls of the temple and might be storage or prayer rooms.

The door directly in front of me led further into the temple, so I turned the knob and slipped inside. Torches flared on the other side, revealing a staircase leading down into the void. Swallowing hard, I started down, the scent of smoke and sacrifice giving way to stale air and something else I couldn't put a finger on. The stairs led down, down, down. I assumed I was underground with the heavy earth pressing around me. Sweat prickled on my neck, and

I had that same odd sense I'd had when I'd been in the crypt.

Vibrations in the air made goose bumps pebble on my arms and when I reached the bottom, I was panting. Arched double doors rose before me, flanked by torches. In the poor light, it was difficult to make out the designs on the doors, but I guessed they were similar to the ones my uncle had caught me examining. Enchanted doors. Oren desperately wanted what was behind them, and a spark of curiosity overrode my fear.

I pressed my palm against stone and searched for a knob, a handle, anything to open the doors with. There was nothing. Even though I could see the crack where the hinges were, the solid mass didn't even reveal a keyhole. My heart sank. The answers were so close, just on the other side of the wall, but I needed magic to access it. If I were a warrior, I'd go upstairs and threaten the priests with my dagger. Didn't Oren say his power would protect me?

The stone shuddered, and I backed away, eyes darting to the shadowed corners. I sprinted toward the blackness just as the doors swung open. Bright, white light blazed and two sorcerers strode out, their long robes whispering against the ground. Instead of golden staffs, both carried vials in their hands and moved swiftly up the stairs.

My mouth went dry with the knowledge of what I had to do. If they caught me, I prayed Oren's magic would protect me. As the doors started to close, I dashed inside and ducked down, making myself small in case anyone was on the other side.

It took my eyes a while to adjust to the brightness, which came from the ceiling. Icicle shaped stalactites hung down, glowing with a blue-white light. It was beautiful, but the light had an odd quality to it. Vibrations hummed, making the hair on my neck stand on end, and I wrinkled my nose against the scent of coopery iron and a faint rot. The cave was crisp, cold, and I rubbed my arms, wondering if I'd descended into the mountainside.

The layout was similar to the temple. Columns thrust toward the ceiling, covered in runes. In front of me on a podium rose the altar, and the halls beyond—lit with that same light—led deeper into the cavern. I'd done it. I'd made it into the vault. And then, with a pang, I realized I was not alone.

I slapped a hand over my mouth to keep from crying out. A creature lay on the altar, staring at me with orb-like eyes. Pressing my back against the wall to make myself smaller, I tried to comprehend what I was seeing.

In the temple, the priests conducted rituals that involved animal sacrifice. Down here, what lay on the altar was vaguely human with two arms and legs attached to an unnaturally skinny, skeletal-like body. The shape of her naked body revealed her to be female. I blinked, rising slowly to my feet as I took in the way she lay—hands and feet bound, blood dripping from a wound in her side, staining the alabaster stone. Her skin was so pale it appeared translucent, and the blood running through her fragile veins wasn't crimson, but dark blue.

She was bald. Either her head had been shaved or her hair had fallen out because of malnourishment. I sucked in a breath when I noticed her ears, pointed, just like Oren's. Her face was heart-shaped, but her eyes were mere orbs of a dull bronze, revealing fear and pain and exhaustion. How was she still alive?

I thought of my uncle's violence—the shock of his slap, the pain of his punch, and the delight in his eyes when he saw blood. Was this what he did? Kept one of the Others under lock and key where no one would find her and used her for sport and pleasure? It was too much to think about, and my stomach twisted for the second time that day, bile rising as dark thoughts scurried around in my mind. My limbs shook and then a voice was in my head.

Help me.

I jerked. Staring. She'd just spoken to me.

"I... I... " I swallowed, cleared my throat, and tried again. "Who are you? Is anyone else here?"

Help me.

The voice came again in my head, slower than before, as if she was losing consciousness. Those orb-like eyes closed and then came one last plea.

Find. The. Piper.

I stumbled back, scanning the hall. I wanted to flee from this horror, but a sudden fury drove me onward. This was wrong.

Conscious of how little time I had, I scanned the area for movement. Magic ran through this haunted dungeon, and I clenched my fists, pulse throbbing as hate for my uncle, the priests, and the sorcerers rose so thick in my throat, it threatened to choke me.

The vibrations became more intense as I walked down a short passage. The light swirled around me as though it were alive, studying me. My unease increased. I shouldn't be here. I needed to run back to natural light and fresh air. Had I truly lived for two years with this horror underneath me? This was the reason bitterness impregnated the palace. No sooner had the thought passed through my mind, the passageway opened up into a nightmare.

High above me hung hundreds of cages, and within each one was one of the Others. They were all stripped naked, male and female, some bleeding, some with arms and legs bent at unnatural angles. Most of them were gaunt, but some had long, lush hair and full figures. The healthy ones had a golden glow about them, a shimmer of life, while the gaunt ones were weary, as though the life had been drained from them.

I waited for a voice in my head, but there was only my silent scream of anguish. How could someone inflict this horror on someone else? And then I understood. These must be the magic-thralls.

Turning on my heel, I fled.

14. Tanith

When I arrived at the doors, they were sealed shut, locking me within. I paced back and forth, trying to calm my racing heartbeat. Think. I had to think, not panic, although what I'd seen I could not be erased from my mind. Broken bones. Slashed skin. I was in a magical torture chamber, and if the sorcerers returned and caught me, what would they do?

The doors had no way of opening, and I did not understand the runes on them. I forced myself to take a deep breath and memorize the shapes to draw for Oren later. At the thought of him, a sob rose in my throat. I wasn't sure how long I stood there, breathing shallowly, when the doors shuddered. A warning.

Wildly, I searched for a place to hide, but with the

blinding light there was none. I dropped into a crouch beside the doors, listening to angry voices as they swung open. My uncle strode in, followed by sorcerers and a few priests.

"Do whatever it takes to stop him," he snarled.

They marched toward the altar without bothering to look around. When the last of them entered, I waited a beat, then caught the door before it closed and dashed out. Sweat dripped down my neck as their argument continued, and I raced up the stairs, two at a time.

At the top, I doubled over in pain, pressing a hand to my chest as I gasped for air. Grateful no one was there to catch me, I crept back into the palace and into chaos. Shouts and cries met my ears. Something jumped on me, and with a squeak, I tossed it off. It was wet, slimy to the touch, and I gaped as I saw the carpeted floor crawling with frogs.

I tried not to step on them, but the creatures kept hopping over my feet, in my hair, on the walls. Each one I tossed off was replaced with more. The beginnings of a headache throbbed in my skull as I sought the exit, my presence ignored as the palace dealt with the crisis. I was almost to the front doors when the howl of a wolf cut through the noise. Oren was waiting for me.

Quickening my pace, I peeked into the wide hall

and instantly pulled back. Guards stood in front of the double doors, blocking the exit. Even the frogs hopping around them weren't enough to discourage them from their duty.

With a groan, I leaned against the wall. Trapped for the second time in one day. What to do? My thoughts reeled, landing on the one way I usually escaped. Retracing my steps, I cut back through the palace, following the winding halls to my old room.

Inside was dark and refreshingly free of frogs. Even the din from the palace was muted within these walls. I started toward the window when a voice made me halt. "Tanith. I hoped you'd return."

Aunt Matzie sat on the bed, her youngest son stretched out beside her, sleeping. Questions tumbled in my head, but the howl from outside came again. I hesitated, torn between leaving or staying to speak with my aunt.

"What's going on?" I asked, shaking a frog out of my hair. It hopped under the bed with an annoyed croak. "I got the book and your message."

"You woke him up and broke the spell of peace. Unless you stop him, there will be war. Faren is stubborn, he will not relent, and neither will the Piper. They will tear this city apart."

"Why?" I demanded, my voice rising to a higher pitch with each word. "Do you know where I've been? Down in the vault, those magical torture chambers, did you know about those?"

"It's not what you think," Aunt Matzie said evenly, almost coldly.

"What is it then?" I bristled. "If you won't tell me, how do you expect me to help?"

She sighed, shoulders wilting as she glanced at her son. Keeping her voice low, she spoke quickly. "There isn't time to explain. You'll have to trust me. Those creatures in the vaults are animals. They aren't human, not like you and I, and if they are released, they will use their magic to obliterate us. If the Piper frees them, they will follow him, look to him as their master, and he has no kindness in his heart, no remorse. Go back with him, find out his secrets and let me know what you discover. If we work together, we can stop him."

"What about the vault? What I saw was inhumane. We don't even treat our animals like that!"

Lifting her shoulders, she pressed her lips together. "Trust me, Tanith. Magic built everything here. It keeps the city alive. I gave you the book to help you understand because you are smarter than I am. If anyone can figure this out, it will be you."

I didn't like that kind of pressure, that belief in my abilities. Pinching the bridge of my nose with my fingers, I tried to calm down and think of a question that would prove useful to me. "When I was in the crypt, I saw a glowing, crystal pyramid. The book did not mention it. What does it mean?"

She sighed. "Tanith, what madness drove you to his tomb?"

Instead of responding, I glanced at the window, waiting for her to go on.

"In history, pyramids are a symbol of resurrection, the return to life after death. As long as he lay undisturbed, the crystal kept him asleep."

Ah, I should have guessed as much. "Now that he's awake, does it carry any power?"

She frowned. "I don't know. If you find it and bring it here, perhaps the sorcerers can spell it again."

I licked my lips, unsure of what to commit to, and moved to the window.

"Tanith, when you have more, find me here."

I nodded, my thoughts a swirl of confusion as I climbed down. Beneath me, frogs wiggled and squirmed, a disturbing mass leaving a sticky residue everywhere they went. Grimacing, I jumped into their midst, squashing them underfoot.

The scream of the death horse made me tense, and I spun as it galloped toward me. It moved with such dizzying speed, I had no time to react as Oren's hand came down and dragged me up in front of him.

He bent low over the horse's back as he sped away from the palace of hidden horrors.

My entire body trembled as he held me and I wanted to close my eyes, but each time I did, I saw that strange creature, bleeding and tied to the altar. What my uncle was doing was wrong, evil, but if my aunt's words were true, the Others would kill us if released. Still, there had to be a way to stop this madness, but I couldn't figure it out and time continued to rush away.

When we arrived back at the castle, Oren was silent. He hauled me off the death horse and held my arm as he escorted me back inside his creepy home. Waves of fury shimmered around him, and I held my tongue. If he was aware of what I'd seen, it would only make him angrier, perhaps desperate. But we needed to talk. I wanted a full explanation, more than what my aunt had told me.

He put me in a chair in front of the fireplace, and I was grateful to sit on something that didn't move. Ironic. I'd enjoyed riding on horseback until I'd met Oren and his skeletal horse. If it weren't warm under my thighs, I might have thought it was a dead thing moving with supernatural speed.

Oren went to the bookshelf and brushed aside odds and ends to reveal a decanter of amber liquid. Taking two crystal glasses, he filled both of them three fingers high, passed me one, and then sat down across from me. He drained his glass in one swallow and I followed his lead. The liquid burned my throat but warmed my belly, and within a few moments, a numbness spread through me.

I examined him, drinking in the hard lines of his masculine jaw, the smoldering anger in his deep-set eyes, and the way he held his broad shoulders, as though he carried the weight of the world. He made a fist, then stretched his slim fingers out, crossing his legs, and then uncrossing them. He looked like an angel in his perfection, a dark angel with tormented eyes.

"I entered the vault," I said.

His eyes snapped to mine, and I detected a glimmer of hope.

"I assume magic seals the doors, and they are covered in runes you might be able to decipher. I snuck in when the sorcerers were coming and going. They keep the magic-thralls down there, but you already knew that, didn't you?"

He nodded once.

I bit my lip and forced myself to go on. If I didn't, he'd make me, for I was his informant. "One of them lay bound to the altar. It was awful. They keep them in cages. Is it true if they go free, their magic will destroy Dowler?"

Oren turned away from me, pinching his chin with his fingers. “They are alive. Did they speak?”

“One did. She sounded as though she was in my mind. She asked me to help and to find… you.”

He squeezed his hand into a fist, then hurled the crystal glass into the fireplace. It shattered and I jumped, surprised by the fury in his movements. He leaned forward, eyes blazing. “It doesn’t matter if they would destroy Dowler, they don’t deserve what is happening to them.”

“Is that why they put you in the tomb all those years ago?” I asked.

His jaw clenched. “I tried to free them once before, this time I will succeed.”

Standing, he marched out of the room.

15. Oren

Outside, I paced backed and forth in the courtyard. I needed to be alone to consider what my next action should be. Summoning bats and frogs was easy, magic born out of impulsive impatience, but turning the waters to blood had taken more thought and drained my magic. I needed something stronger to persuade Lord Faren, something the sorcerers could not unravel in a matter of hours. Each time I cast a spell, they crafted a counter-spell. The waters were clear again, and by the end of the night, the frogs would be gone too. At least they would have done their irksome duty, instilling fear among the people.

Tanith's confession only made my fury grow. Secretly, I'd hoped it might be over and that I'd slept through the evil that lurked beneath the palace. But the plight of the magic-thralls had only gotten worse. What made their situation a nightmare was that even though they decayed, they were like me —undying.

Now that I was back, time was of the essence to save them, and Tanith—my eyes and ears on the inside—had given me a clue. The doors were sealed with magic. I paced as the semblance of an idea came to me. Sealed. By Magic. But not the thrall's magic, no. It must be the joint power of the sorcerers. I'd never entered the vault because the collective power of the sorcerers and the rock that lined the cave walls were my undoing. It made me weak and my will slipped away while their voices in my head grew stronger. I needed Lord Faren to give his word and allow the thralls to go free because I could not enter the vault and save them myself.

I walked to the barn, considering Tanith's words. She'd asked if the thralls would destroy Dowler when they were free. At first, they'd be too weak to do much of anything, but they were a powerful race. Their strength would return and then, perhaps, they'd seek revenge, and I did not have the power to control them with my flute. But the people of Dowler deserved retribution for what they'd done or turned a blind eye to. The rot in the city was impossible to ignore. Even Tanith knew that all was not as it should be.

Her desire to flee was right, and I could not fault her for it, only the way she went about it. Unfortunately for her, even if she met the terms of the deal I'd set between us, I had no way of financing her journey to Solynn. The riches I had were in the crypt and they were cursed by magic. Better to remain there than see the light of day. All except for the crystal pyramid which I'd locked away.

Inside the barn, I put a rope around the donkey's neck and led the creature out to the forge. It would take a while for it to heat, but I secured the donkey to the wheel that fed the fire and gathered materials. My clever idea just might work. In the meantime, I'd consider another blight to torture Lord Faren.

I threw myself into the work, unaware of time. Humans carried many assumptions about immortals, assuming long life made us callous, magic made us cruel, or our hearts were hollow drums, beating for no reason. In truth, I keenly sensed more, and it left me craving that elusive emotion humans called love. I desired a partnership that combined the needs of the mental and physical into something indescribable.

My lovely wife was a welcome distraction, but although flares of heat passed between us, we were far from single-minded. The only bond we had was a vow she had no intention of keeping. Still, I relished her tiny gasps when I got close to her, the taste of her silky lips, the way her eyes widened when I touched her. Through it all, she hadn't broken down or sobbed or begged, even though I was forcing her to choose between her family and my needs.

A bolt of forbidden desire passed through me as I thought of her and I stood, suddenly realizing I'd been working for hours. Was that the glimmer of the sun seeping through the windows? Had it been a day, two days, that I'd left her alone in the castle?

I stared at the cooling iron, still hot to the touch. Lifting it with the tongs, I put it back in a box, and leaving the donkey chewing on hay, headed back to the castle.

More animals were around now. I sensed their presence and saw their tiny footprints in the mud. A few deer had passed by, some rabbits, and the barn would have more of my familiars. Loneliness had made me single-minded, and even the animals and my stone servants did not make up for the lack of contact with others. I was sure Tanith would be upset unless she'd managed to run away. And there was also that unwelcome house guest I'd forgotten about.

16. TANITH

After Oren left, I took a bath. I hurried, unsure of when he'd return, but grateful to wash the filth from my body. If only I could wash away what I'd seen in the vault. Part of me wanted to understand what the sorcerers were doing, but the other part of me, the stronger part, wanted to run. Even though earlier that same day I'd decided this was my fault and I had to fix it, as I scrubbed my skin in the tub, I concluded it was far too big and too dangerous of a task for me.

What if Oren's protection didn't work, and the sorcerers caught me? Would they strip me down, tie me to the altar, and bleed me? Knowing my uncle, he'd do nothing to stop them, and with his appetite for violence, might even participate. After all, he'd let me marry the Devil of Dowler. I shivered as I remembered the way Oren had hurled the glass into the fireplace, shattering on the stone. Unlike my uncle, Oren didn't use his strength for abuse. I recalled his arm around my waist, the way his fingers had brushed my thigh when he'd discovered the knife, and the way he'd kissed me on our wedding night. My skin flushed hot and threads of desire coursed through me. It was all too much, too fast.

After bathing, I awoke Pip to keep me company for the rest of the day, aware of the absurdity of relying on a hideous stone statue for comfort. In actuality, I just wanted a hug. Rubbing my nose, I thought of my parents and our home full of love and laughter. My mother's soothing hugs, my father's infectious laughter. That was where I belonged, but ever since the carriage accident, nothing had been the same.

Mother had passed quickly, but father had lingered in unimaginable pain. On his deathbed, he had me send a letter to his brother, and now I wondered if father had known the dark history of Dowler. As soon as he was of age, he'd run away from home and left his brother, ten years his elder, to rule the city. My father made a name for himself in Solynn, and the first I'd heard of Dowler was when he'd asked for help, unwilling to leave me alone. It was no use feeling sorry for myself, but grief had clouded my judgement. If I'd been thinking clearly then, I would have rejected the invitation to Dowler, stayed in Solynn, and figured out my finances for myself.

Oren did not return that evening. Slightly irritated with him for leaving me alone, I shut myself in my room, both disconcerted and relieved when I discovered it had no lock. While it was easy for me to escape, it would also be simple for someone to enter my room. Even with the knife under my pillow and Pip resting at the foot of the bed, I did not feel safe.

Eventually, I drifted off to sleep and a nightmare full of blood, smoke, and sacrifice filled my mind. I woke with a start, sweating, pulse racing, and sat up, pulling the covers up to my chin. "Pip," I whispered. "I need light."

I heard his obedient thump as he hopped off the bed and trotted to the fireplace. A tiny flicker appeared, gaining strength, and I relaxed. Funny how light made everything seem okay, while the darkness was terrifying. "Thank you," I told him, patting the bed. "You can come back up here now."

He joined me, nose nuzzling against my hand. I

petted him to soothe my nerves, still unused to the coolness of his stone body.

A thud came from above me and I stiffened, my eyes drawn to the ceiling. It came again, followed by a cry—more like a squeak of terror, quickly snuffed out. Heart pounding, I snatched my dagger and held it in both hands, pulling my knees up to my chest. Eyes wild, I waited, wondering if Oren was back and sneaking around the castle, causing chaos at night. But the sound did not come again, and finally, I went back to sleep.

Oren did not return the next day, and I found myself unable to focus on anything but the idea of escape. Once again, my attempt to leave by walking out was thwarted by the staircases that only led up, leaving me to my last resort. Back in the room, Pip, my guard, didn't stop me from yanking off the bedcovers and tying the sheets into knots. First, I stripped Oren's bed, because I was angry with him, and then my bed. Although I knew little about knots, I made them as tight as possible, creating a makeshift rope before taking it out to the balcony. I tied one end around the railings, tugging on it to ensure it would hold my weight. The rope only went halfway down, but I'd used all the sheets, and when I asked Pip for rope, he stared at me blankly. Likely not allowed to help me escape.

I packed the satchel with clothes, put my cloak around my shoulders, and wrapped the remains of my lunch in a napkin. There was a trail through the woods, and if I followed it during daylight, I'd be fine. There was still the matter of money, but I could sell my clothes, trade, or barter. My first step was escaping the castle. When at last I was ready, I tossed the satchel over the balcony, watching it fall to the ground with a bang. There. One step done.

Taking a deep breath, I swung my legs over the balcony, holding tight to the railings, hoping my makeshift rope would work. If it didn't, I was dead, but it was better than wasting away in the castle, waiting for Oren to return. Two days wasn't long, but I was impatient and after what I'd seen in the vault, I didn't want to be caught in a battle of magic between Oren and Lord Faren.

Fisting the sheet in my hand, I tugged on it, testing my weight. It held, so I slowly lowered myself down. Instead of looking at the ground, I kept my gaze on the balcony, and Pip wagging his tail, as though he was happy I was escaping. It was hard to read his expression since only his eyes changed, but I liked to think he was pleased with my cleverness.

Halfway down, the sheets started to rip, and I froze, arms straining, feet dangling. I searched the railing and immediately saw that while my knots held, my weight was tearing my rope ladder. Swallowing hard, I moved, but the sheet ripped further and I dropped fast. I came to a sudden stop, swaying dangerously in the wind, the ground still two stories below me.

If I didn't catch hold of something, I'd fall to my death. Suppressing a moan, I brought one hand down, my entire body straining with effort. Sweat dripped off my neck as the sun beat down, hot and relentless. I moved another hand, holding my breath. It was working. I was moving.

Lowering myself hand over hand, I forced myself to think positive thoughts. The tear had made my rope ladder longer. Soon I'd reach the ground and dash off into the forest. The tales of people being lost in the woods were just that, a fable. All I needed to do was follow the trail, and I'd reach the city before nightfall. I took a slow breath, unable to keep my hands from trembling. The knot holding the sheet to the railing gave way with a gentle whooshing sound, and I fell.

I stretched out my arms, too surprised to cry out as wind rushed by, tugging at me like fingers, as if it could stop the pull of gravity. A sweet sound rushed to my ears, the call of a flute. What a pleasant sound to listen to as I plummeted to my death. Still, my body went rigid as I braced myself for impact, and the world around me slowed—the stones of the castle, the foliage of the trees, the beams of sunlight, and fat, lazy clouds. Maybe this was what death was like, knowing it would be over soon and finding a sudden appreciation for life. I waited for a sob to break. Instead, I landed on something hard and sprawled on the ground.

My first thought was that the fall didn't hurt nearly as much as I expected it to. My second was that I was alive, and nothing was broken. Hands clamped around my arms and dragged me to my feet. I looked up into Oren's scowling face and my heart sank. No, no, no. I hadn't come this far to be recaptured by my jailer. I'd just felt proud of myself for escaping.

"What madness possessed you to do such a thing?" he snapped, his eyes going from me to the balcony, to the rope of sheets, which lay like a dead snake on the ground.

"You were gone for two days," I retorted. "I didn't think you were coming back, so I decided to leave. And your enchanted castle won't let me out."

He glowered at me, eyes dark. "That was idiotic. You forced me to save you with my flute."

Ah, the music. Of course it had been him, but I wasn't ready to forgive or forget, and his anger made me bristle. “This wouldn’t have happened if you hadn’t left me alone.”

“This wouldn’t have happened if you hadn’t tried to escape. I made a deal with you, but somehow it’s not good enough. Is it?”

“It’s too much,” I protested as he snatched up my bag and ushered me around the castle. “Your plan is impossible. I’m only human, not meant to get in the middle of a magical war.”

“That’s not what this is about,” he said tightly, pausing as his foot hit something that lay on the ground.

He bent to pick it up, and my heart sank as I realized it was the leather journal my aunt had given me. Dropping the satchel, he picked it up, frowning as it fell open.

My heart raced, and I was grateful I’d burned the note from my aunt but unsure how he’d react.

When he spoke, his voice was quiet. “This is yours, isn’t it?”

What else could I say? “Yes.”

His amber eyes blazed as they went from me to the book, to the satchel, and I watched as he put the pieces together. “Your aunt gave you this, and the knife, and what else? Did she ask you to find out all my secrets? Learn about magic so you could turn me over to them?”

Each word cut like a knife, as if I were betraying him. I didn't know what to think or say. Mutely, I allowed him to take me back to the castle, feeling his wrath simmer. It was only when we were inside that he released me, jaw working as he glared at me.

"Oren." I used his name in a half-hearted attempt to soothe him. "It's not what you think."

17. TANITH

Oren's gaze smoldered with an inner fire. His mouth pressed into a firm line and his nostrils flared as he glared at me. "You attempt to try my patience at every turn when I'm only protecting you from what could happen. But you don't care, do you? As long as you get your way, as long as you escape. Let me tell you what happens to those who don't heed my warning."

He lunged, snatching my wrist, and pulled me down the hall. I let myself be hurried along, aware I had nothing left to say. He knew my secret. He'd caught me, and saying I was sorry was inefficient when my blatant actions displayed my lack of repentance.

"What are you going to do with me?" I begged as we climbed the spires into the heights of the castle.

He did not answer, only kept moving until I was breathless, almost running behind him. Finally, we reached a gloomy hall, thick with layers of dust, cobwebs almost concealing the flickering candlelight. Oren swung open a door and pushed me inside.

The slanted roof of the attic let in sunlight, clearly displaying layers of dust and dirt. A rocking chair, crisscrossed with spiderwebs, sat in the center of the room, and in it sat a corpse wearing a faded yellow dress. All the flesh was gone, leaving only bone with a grinning skull, and eyes sockets staring into endless blackness. Terror seized me.

I spun, intending to run, but Oren caught me, trapping my arms as he forced me to stare at death. His free hand squeezed my jaw and his lips feathered my ear as he whispered. "Look. This could be you."

"What did you do?" I arched my back, panic screaming in my mind: Fight. Escape. Run. "Who is she?"

"My wife."

Those two words drilled through me, and my legs buckled. He'd had a wife. He had been married before. An irritating sort of envy turned my panic into fury. "What are you going to do? Kill me like you killed her?" I struggled in his grip, but I wasn't getting away, he was deceptively strong.

"I'd always been fond of my wife, but she refused to listen to me, too stubborn to let me protect her. She died by her own hand."

"You mean you murdered her?" I spat. "Why keep her here, locked up in the attic?"

Oren let go of me so swiftly, I almost fell down. Instead of letting me escape, he backed me up against the wall, his body pressing against mine, so close I felt the heat pouring off him in waves. Dizzy, I struggled to breathe. I couldn't let him affect me like this, but his hard expression taunted me. He bared his sharp teeth, searching my face for what? A sign of contriteness?

"I did not keep her locked up because I wanted to. She made herself a toxic potion and drank it. It killed her, and then they captured me and buried me alive."

Oh. That was not what I expected. "Did you love her?"

"Love." He snorted. "Our marriage was arranged. I took those vows seriously, but love? Nay. I was rather fond of her, just like I'm fond of you."

"Really?" I lashed out, spitting his words back in his face. "If you're so fond of me, why keep me here? Force me to do your bidding? Why don't you let me go free?"

"Because you committed a crime and there are consequences for such actions," he snarled. "You can't do something wrong and then walk away as if it didn't happen. You reap the benefits of what you sow in life."

"I'm not a gardener," I quipped at his analogy. "And who made you the judge of me?"

"You did the moment you walked into the crypt and took what did not belong to you."

My pulse raced and tension coiled deep within my belly. With each word, he moved closer until our noses were mere inches apart.

I glared up at him, jaw set, unable to miss the flecks of gold dust that flashed in his eyes. "Men cannot judge me," I protested weakly.

"I'm inhuman, you know this," he growled in return.

I took a shuddering breath, unable to get enough air with him pressing against me. I was furious. He'd caught me escaping, found the journal, assumed I meant to betray him, showed me his dead wife, told me he didn't love me, and continued to punish me for my actions. But there was something else mounting between us, and I knew, as my gaze flickered to his lips, it was that undeniable attraction. He lured me in. The feelings that surged through me were confusing and dark, and so to keep my guard up and protect myself, I responded with unkindness. “True, but I’m your new wife, and you don’t act like you’re fond of me.”

His jaw tightened and his hands moved quickly, threading through my curls with surprising gentleness for the speed at which he moved. He tilted my head until it was impossible to move away, the fever of heat between us rising to a new level. Warning blazed in his amber eyes as he searched my face.

I swallowed hard, a small gasp escaping my throat. I was sure he could hear my heart thudding like a drum in my chest, booming against his. The juncture between my legs ached as the tension in my belly coiled even tighter.

And then his lips were on mine. Liquid heat spiked between us, turning molten. My eyes closed of their own accord and my lips parted. This was what I’d been waiting for.

My fingers gripped the back of his shirt, pulling him closer to me as I turned my head to taste him and opened my mouth for more. He devoured me with his kiss, his serpentine tongue thrusting into my mouth, possessing me, stealing my breath. I pushed against him but he pushed back, fingers tightening in my hair as the kissed turned urgent.

My core fluttered with the need for release, and I moaned into him.

Keeping me pinned to the wall, he pressed his knee between my legs, and shamelessly, I thrust myself against him, resentful of the fabric that blocked me from feeling too much. I could drown in this kiss, I could live in it, for I had no doubt it was the kind of hot kiss that had power over life or death.

I could not deny the sparks of arousal, nor the way lust flared between us. Was it so wrong to be hungry and wet for my husband?

Just like that, he broke the kiss. Pressing a hand against my belly, he leaned into me, his lips grazing my ear. "I smell your arousal. You want me deep inside you. This turns you on and now you know, little wife, I'm quite fond of you. But until you admit you accept the consequences of your actions, nothing else will happen between us."

"Then you punish yourself too." I gasped, chest heaving as I sucked in air.

In response, he bit down on my lower lip, so hard he drew blood. His tongue skimmed my mouth, and I sighed, leaning against him for support.

An apology rose on the tip of my tongue. Anything to keep the delightful sensations that buzzed through me, curated by his touch.

Stepping away, he broke all contact and strode down the hall. I watched until he was out of sight, then sagged against the wall, pressing one hand to my lips as though I could hold his kiss of fire inside.

18. Tanith

Back in the room, Oren sat in front of the fire, drinking and ignoring the ruined bed. He studied me as I approached, then waved a hand, motioning for me to join him. "Tanith, we need to talk."

My initial reaction was to taunt him, but the softening expression on his face made the unkind words melt away. I sat down heavily, my knees still weak from his feverish kisses. Threads of confusion went through me at his mannerisms. How could he be so cold and cruel, and yet so hot and handsome? He wielded magic relentlessly, determined to punish the city until he got what he wanted, and try as I might, I could not completely blame him for it.

"Speak. I'm listening," I said, with none of my former haughtiness lacing my words.

"Not here." Oren stood, eyeing the destroyed bed. "I've asked the butler, Rone, to prepare a sitting room for us. He and his staff of gargoyles will clean up the castle, especially in here. I'm sure you're tired of being stuck in these rooms."

I breathed out slowly. Why was Oren being kind to me? "It is tiresome," I admitted. "I'm used to more freedoms."

His lips curved up in a wry smile. "Ironic, that you would use the word freedom. Come, stubborn wife of mine, I believe we need to start being honest with each other."

Standing in front of me, he held out his hand. I hesitated before taking it, my breath hitching at the contact. He tucked my hand under his arm and escorted me from the room, like a lady going to a ball.

I snuck glances at him as he took me back downstairs, and the truth weighed heavy on my conscience. He was so handsome it hurt, like some dark angel I'd found in a tomb and brought back to life. I'd seen his dark side and the fury he unleashed with his flute, yet with me, his reactions were unusual. I'd tried to escape, and he'd shown me his dead wife and threatened me with … kisses. Was he truly fond of me? I was supposed to be a tool to do his bidding. A thief, a spy, nothing more. But what if I wanted to be more?

The idea popped into my mind, and the ridiculousness of it almost made me laugh. It had barely been a week, and already, I entertained notions and ideas I'd never have considered in Solynn. Although I had to admit, I'd always been curious. My first kiss had been during a ball. A young lord had engaged me in a dance, then led me outside to the gardens, even though the rules of society forbade us—the unmarried—to be alone together. We'd exchanged kisses in the dark, laughing and giggling before returning. I'd enjoyed it, and curious, I went further and further until my suitor, George.

We were going to get married. He made me laugh, teased me mercilessly, and was always getting into mischief with his friends. Sometimes I thought he preferred them over me, but mother had said that sometimes love comes softly—or not at all.

When my parents died, George grew awkward and distant. He promised to write while I grieved in Dowler, but I had never heard from him. Our relationship had been light, fun, and so when something serious happened, neither of us knew how to handle it. At least not together. I had nothing but kind feelings and thoughts towards sweet George. He'd been slightly pudgy, fumbling and awkward, but always zealous about making love. He was the only man I'd been with, but compared to Oren, he seemed like a boy.

Oren, my husband, hadn't once asked me to strip off my clothes for him. My entire body flushed with the fact that I wanted him to peel off my clothes, claim me with his tongue, his lips, his fingers—his cock. What was he waiting for? I knew he was attracted to me, for the way he kissed me was no lie. In fact, my lips were still swollen from his love bites earlier.

We came to a stop under a carved doorway, and I gasped as little gargoyles—only three or four feet tall—scurried about. There were perhaps half a dozen of them, some more animal, others more human. Each one had a pair of wings—some tiny, as if just for looks, and others large and swooping as if, despite being stone, they'd fly away. They looked up when we approached, their tiny orbs all different colors—ebony, topaz, gold, maroon, turquoise. One by one, they bowed and left, except for the last one. He looked like a goblin, at least from drawings I'd seen in storybooks.

"Thank you, Rone," Oren said. "Have the suite cleaned and dinner sent up at a quarter past six. That will be all."

Rone padded away while I gawked after him.

"They don't speak. What if they have something to say?"

Oren smirked. "They are re-animated stone, but their thoughts transfer to me. They belong to the castle, and when I'm gone, they'll return to stone again."

"What if they want the chance to live?" I asked, my thoughts going back to the thralls in the vault. They didn't have a choice in what happened to them, and neither did the gargoyles. Was that fair?

"I'm not a Creator. I use magic, but I cannot breathe life into stone and make it live forever. To create life, one must have a soul. Once there was a knight who aspired to become a Creator, but when he put soul into his creations, they turned into monsters. Which makes one consider, what is the essence of a soul, and why can't it be taken from one vessel and moved to another, empty vessel? What makes the created turn into monsters, when the creator can be pure? Or are we all drawn towards darkness, lured by the dusk, the grayness between good and evil? If so, perhaps we're all simply looking for a way to exist without consequences, to do what we want to do without regard for the ripples it will cause in this life and the life to come."

"You're saying that a soul makes one truly alive,

and that the gargoyles only live here because of the enchantment of magic?"

"Yes, but I did not bring you here to talk about my musings. Although given the contents of the book your aunt gave you, perhaps you might be interested."

His voice took on an edge I did not care for, and I stiffened, dragging my gaze from the angles of his flawless face back to the room.

It was a lounge, perhaps the same one he'd taken me to the night I'd awakened him. With the furniture uncovered and the dust and cobwebs gone, I couldn't be sure. Letting go of his arm, I flounced further in, taking in the chairs and sofas, low-lying tables arranged in a way to attract the heat from the fire. The heavy curtains were pulled back and a chandelier twinkled above me, its diamonds catching and reflecting the sunlight into rainbow-like prisms that decorated each wall.

I noted the food and wine set out on a table, and only when Oren closed the doors with a thump did I face him again. "I am rather interested in your thoughts," I quipped. "Not necessarily philosophy, but life, creation, and magic are all curiosities that the professors in Solynn do not have the expertise to lecture about."

Hands behind his back, he glided further into the

room, finally resting with his elbow on the mantle while he poked at the fire. It hissed back at him and flared up brighter. "Not much has changed then. There are still lectures and professors who believe themselves above all others because of their knowledge, their ability to decipher the hidden meaning in books. But what about experience? Have they gone out and lived, found truth and knowledge for themselves before returning to impart the wisdom they've gained?"

Shrugging, I made myself a plate of food and settled down at the table with a glass full of a dark-colored wine. I tested it on my tongue, pleased that it tasted like blackberries and apples. "I never asked about their personal experiences. The stories they told were more entertaining than enlightening, but they did not dwell on the fantastical, just the basics of life in Solynn."

"Solynn," he repeated, waving his hand. "This city you're so impatient to get back to. Why?"

I took a bite of a tart, staring at his side profile while I chewed. How was he so devastatingly and utterly handsome? My stomach shouldn't flip when I looked at him, and yet, it did. "Anywhere is better than here." The words came out vicious.

His amber gaze descended on me, but shadows haunted his eyes. The fire only lit part of his face, making his long hair glisten while the rest of him stayed shrouded in darkness. A delicious shiver of desire went through me, and I dropped my eyes, no longer interested in finishing my pastry.

"Tanith, if you want to leave, you need to make a choice. Will you assist me as my spy, or will you betray me to your aunt and uncle?"

I dropped the pastry, unnerved with the deadly calm in his tone and unable to miss the coldness in his gaze—a far cry from the way he'd kissed me. To give myself more time to answer, I took a sip of wine. "Why do you force me to choose when I don't understand exactly what I'm choosing? Besides, when you first captured me, you gave me no choice."

"Now I am, and you resent me for it?"

"I need to know more before I decide. You said you were going to be honest with me."

"What does your heart say?"

I grimaced. "My heart says nothing. Besides it doesn't matter how I feel. I have to use logic to make a choice, not rely on emotions."

His lips curled. Leaving his spot by the fire, he drifted closer to me. "Why? Because emotions are unreliable, and your head will keep you on the straight and narrow path?"

"I don't know what you're talking about," I retorted with a scowl. "Emotions change. They are unreliable, don't you know? Or perhaps you don't have a heart."

He pressed his hand to his chest, somehow opening his shirt even wider. My face flushed, but I did not look away. "I always rely on my emotions to guide me. Perhaps that's the difference between you and me, mortal and immortal. In fact, all my senses are heightened, which allows me to make better decisions."

"Is that why you're plaguing the citizens of Dowler? Because you're better than us, mere humans?"

Instead of reacting to my words, he raised an eyebrow. "Did you read the book your aunt gave you?"

"Yes," I muttered, swallowing down the last of the wine. "I did not fully understand it. It was more of a history of the origins of the Creator, the divines, and other great ones with powerful magic that was lost when mortals took over the world."

"Ah. It is an old text, not to be taken at face value, but the more you read and re-read it, the more you'll understand the hidden messages within the book. I assume your aunt studied at the temple with the priests, or with Lord Faren, which is how she came to understand the deep truths and hold to her stance."

I pressed my lips together, recalling my sudden and sharp anger when she'd said the creatures in the vault weren't human, but mere animals to mistreat. Taking a deep breath, I reminded myself that, before my failed attempt at fleeing, I'd decided I had a part to play in saving Dowler. But from whom? Oren's magic, or Lord Faren's heavy-handed anger?

"I know little about my aunt, but does our original deal still stand? If I help you, you'll let me go free?"

"Yes, the marriage will be void. However, are you agreeing to help me so that you can gain my secrets and betray me to your aunt and uncle?"

Lifting my chin, I held his gaze. "In the interest of being honest, I'm not sure what to think. What I saw in the vault horrified me. It was worse than anything I'd imagined. However, my aunt's concern is valid. The magic-thralls are powerful, are they not? And if we free them, won't they use magic for revenge and destroy Dowler?"

Oren prowled closer to my chair, like a predator about to strike. "In the interest of being honest, Tanith, I will destroy Dowler if they are not freed."

That edge of dangerous anger was back, the hints of unnamable fury. And I believed him. Swallowing hard, I voiced the concern I kept coming back to. "What about the people of Dowler? The innocents?"

"They are guilty by association. They made their home in the belly of the wicked, and if they do not leave, they will be judged."

"That's not fair," I protested, although the words shriveled up in my mouth. How presumptuous of me to think of fairness when nothing concerning Oren could be categorized into the black and white mortal buckets of right and wrong.

"No, it's not fair, but they are free to leave, free to save themselves. I have warned them. They've seen what is to come. Dowler is doomed. It will be destroyed. No matter what happens, you'll have to stand by and accept that or be proactive and help me. I don't have to give you a choice, for you made yourself mine the moment you stepped into my tomb."

The word *mine* sent a velvet shiver through my lower belly, and I tilted my head back as he paused behind me. His hand dropped to my shoulder and squeezed, confirming his claim and something else. Desire? My heart kicked, and we remained frozen, my gaze on his, aware that the way I tilted my head back left my throat bare. His searching eyes skimmed over my skin as though he could read my future.

My thoughts turned into a haze of confusion, and the words that jumped to my lips were impulse driven, inspired by his touch. "You say I'm yours.

You took me as your wife, and yet, you've never invited me to your bed."

I wished those words unsaid the moment they left my mouth. Oren's hand left my shoulder as he stepped back, just as astonished as I was.

19. Tanith

Oren sank into the chair beside me, a wry smile on his face. Gliding his slim fingers through his hair, he tucked it behind his pointed ears as he regarded me. "Is that what you want? An invitation to my bed? Even though you also want the marriage annulled? What a contradiction."

The laughter in his tone did not reassure me and my hand trembled as I refilled my wineglass. "I don't know why I said that. I didn't mean …"

"It was rather honest of you." He chuckled, taking the wine bottle from my hand and pouring himself a glass. "Look at me, Tanith, and I will tell you the truth."

It was hard to turn my head, for I was very much aware of the immortal being who sat beside me, promising to destroy a city at his whim, and then laughing when I complained about our marital bed. What had possessed me to say such a thing?

My clothes were too tight, restricting, my face hot, and the wine didn't help at all. I needed something to cool me down. But more than anything, I wanted to sink into the ground instead of facing him.

Oren didn't give me a choice. His fingers curved around my chin, turning it toward him. His touch would be my undoing, and I noted the way his hand lingered on my skin before he released me. Nothing in his eyes made me think he meant to taunt me or laugh at me, and his expression, one of blatant curiosity, was more than I deserved.

He spoke slowly, as if afraid of hurting me. "I did not explain because I assumed you would not be interested. After all, this is a marriage of convenience."

I frowned. Who exactly was this marriage convenient for? But I swallowed down my words, determined to hear him out.

"I'm not mortal, and although I have human tendencies, I am different."

How? I willed myself not to look down at his pants because that would not give me an answer. But I feared maybe he was deformed—odd, unusually large, or small, and embarrassed by what he lacked or couldn't do.

As if he sensed my thoughts, he glanced at the fire. "I'm not explaining this well. Tanith, you are welcome in my bed any time you please, but beyond kissing, we can go no further. Not because I don't want to, but I have to restrain myself. If you and I … if we are intimate, I will change you."

Eyes narrowed, I studied him. This was the most awkward conversation I'd ever had and yet …. "How? Are you going to kill me?"

He shook his head. "Quite the opposite, in fact. When mortals come together, it's for two reasons, for pleasure or to procreate. There is an exchange that allows new life to grow."

"Yes, I know how it works." I stopped just short of rolling my eyes.

"But with humans, that new life is a child, and while it is possible for an inhuman and a human to have children, what often happens during intimate moments …" Breaking off mid-sentence, he sighed. "You'll become like me, inhuman."

I licked my lips, which were suddenly dry. "I'd be immortal?"

"Correct."

"But not when kissing, only when being intimate?"

He nodded, eyes hard again. “It is not a fate anyone would want. I had no choice, and I would not accidentally force immortality onto someone else.”

“Oh.” I breathed, curious. Unable to stop myself, I added, “Does it happen instantly or over a progression of time?”

Folding his arms over his chest, he leaned back, regarding me. “Tanith, you curious creature, you tempt me with your words, but no, we will not test it out to see if you will become immortal. Trust me on this.”

“Trust doesn’t come easily,” I retorted, settling back into our old territory of banter now that the awkward conversation was over.

Although it left me with a sourness in the pit of my belly. Not that I’d wanted to have sex with him, but now that he’d told me no, suddenly, it was exactly what I craved. But I’d wallow in self-pity another time, for this afternoon was all about gaining answers. I stared at my lap to hide my disappointment, but when his hand landed on my thigh, I faced him, eyes wide.

“You seem upset,” he said.

“I’m not,” I snapped. More words rushed to mind, but I did not say them out loud.

Ignoring my outburst, Oren continued. “I don’t expect to earn your trust quickly, but I will communicate more. Sometimes I get swept away in my work, and I forget about things you'd consider normal—eating, drinking, sleeping. The drive to finish what I started propels me on. But now when I leave, I'll take you with me, and you can remind me of those basic needs."

I nodded, grateful he'd changed the topic, but his hand on my thigh was warm and tantalizing after our discussion about what was forbidden.

"I was gone so long because I made you something. But Tanith, I need you to go back into the vault."

I crossed my arms and waited, tamping down the slight twitch of anticipation.

He held out his hand, revealing a bronze skeleton key, small but elegantly designed. He'd even taken the time to fasten a leather cord around it, creating a necklace.

"What is it for?"

"This key will unlock anything you come across, even magical items."

"Ah, something useful for while I'm sneaking around the palace."

Oren held up the necklace. "Yes, will you allow me?"

I nodded, pulling my hair to one side as he moved behind me and knotted the key around my throat, warm fingers grazing my neck. Unable to help myself, I sucked in a breath, inhaling his woodsy scent, then shivered as the cold metal touched my bare skin. I held up the key and ran my fingers over the grooves. "You made this? Were you a blacksmith in another life? First a tailor, and now this?"

"I learned a trick or two during my days, although it should not have taken me so long to make it. When I sink into a task, I often lose track of time." He trailed off, for he'd already apologized.

I marveled at the key a bit longer before putting it down, my stomach twisting at the idea of entering the vault again.

"Tomorrow, we return to the city," Oren explained. "Speak with your aunt, find out more about the runes in the vault, get a copy of them if you can. I need to see them in order to break the magic, and as you know, I can't go down there myself."

My attempt to memorize the runes hadn't gone well, and after entering the vault, all I had thought about was escape. "Oren," I protested. "What if the sorcerers and priests catch me? I believe the answer to what you seek lies in the temple, but it's only a matter of time. The other day was pure luck."

"No, it wasn't." He moved to the edge of his seat.

"Why do you think I made you these clothes? They blend into the walls, into shadows, so you aren't likely to be seen. And my magic protected you. The vow we spoke did its work."

I closed my mouth because there didn't seem to be another option. "I don't like it," I grumbled.

He leaned closer until I could taste the apples on his breath. "You still have a choice to make."

And then he pulled away, leaving me breathless and angsty.

He strode about the room, restless. It reminded me of when the circus came to Solynn, and the creatures paced in cages, leaving me wondering if they desired to be free. I bit my lower lip, studying the gracefulness and power of Oren's movements, as though he were one of those wild beasts waiting for liberation.

When he spoke, I stilled, lost in the intonation of his musical voice.

"In the beginning, the Creator designed the celestial and the mundane. That's how it all began. Magic spread throughout the world, freely given, until mortals and immortals alike abused it. Their deeds caused darkness and evil abound. Oppression and unfairness spread liberally, and the inhabitants of this world turned their back on the Creator, the very one who gave them life, who gave them everything.

They trusted more in the work of their hands than what faith, belief, and magic could provide. They used science and innovation, the laws of nature, to overrule the Creator's designs, and they were allowed to do so, for we have free will to decide our fate. But in the darker corners of the world, the quieter places, magic still abounds and Others dwell in the shadows where none can capture and study them for science. In those remote places, unusual things happen because of such magic."

I clasped my hands in my lap, sensing he was about to tell me things I'd never heard before. His first words were like the journal, but perhaps the text was at a level that went over my head. He was right. I'd have to read and re-read it to comprehend it fully, but his words were a clue to the mystery of what was happening in Dowler.

"Magic became elusive, and few understood how to capture and wield it for their own means. Often, the unexplained would happen, and it usually involved music. Thus, those who wanted to use great magic turned to music as a way to draw power to them and use it for their own means. Magical users have many names—wizard, enchantress, sorcerer, musician. Once a sorcerer made plants grow with only his voice. Another summoned spirits with his violin, and others opened portals into undiscovered lands, allowing mortals and immortals to come and go as they pleased. I am no more unique than any of them, and sometimes I wonder what happened to them. Whether they overcame their dark pursuits."

"Did all of them—the magic users—turn evil?" I asked, for his words suggested the dark trajectory of their deeds.

He faced me, arms crossed, wavering before he said, "Yes."

I sucked in a deep breath. "Would you say that you are evil too?"

A dark chuckle rumbled in his throat. "It depends on who you speak to. Magic causes change, power can go to the head. A long, long time ago, I made mistakes and I'm forced to endure the repercussions of those mistakes."

When he ceased speaking, a shadow fell over his face, revealing a hollowness that made my heart ache. Had the years of his life been kind to him, or did he prefer to return to his coffin and sleep in blissful unawareness? I supposed mortality was a blessing—at least one day I'd die, and while that thought was morbid, it was also a relief. I wouldn't have to keep going on and on and on endlessly.

For the first time, I thought I might understand my dangerous, devilish captor and why his actions were so extreme. It was no excuse for what he'd done, and what he was doing now, but it cast a bit of light into the darkness. He was driven to free the magic-thralls because they were all he had. And once they were free, then what? Would he go back to sleep? Channel his anger toward something else?

If I were a good wife, I'd comfort him and promise to follow his rules, but he was a maniac, hell bent on destruction. If I didn't stop him, who would? After all, I'd been the one to wake him. Instead of running, I should put him back to sleep where he couldn't hurt anyone anymore.

My conscience pricked at me still though, for without the Piper, who had the power to save the magic-thralls?

20. Tanith

Despite how many times we'd dashed through the city on Oren's nightmare horse, I'd never grow used to the terrifying sensation that gripped me as it moved—wings spread, muscled bunched, legs elongated, and Oren's arm around my waist, holding me tight.

We burst into the courtyard, the repaired gates open to welcome us. He swung off the horse, taking me with him. When my feet touched the ground, I expected him to let go, but instead his arm tightened, pulling me closer until our faces were mere inches away. I flushed under his scrutiny but did not back down. "Don't get caught," he whispered gruffly, his breath feathering my lips.

Desire stirred inside me, along with a cold

reminder of our conversation yesterday and the echo of his words—*I'm quite fond of my wife.*

Instead of flinging a taunt back at him, I held his amber gaze. "I won't."

His jaw worked, as though he would say more, but he promptly released me. Without hesitation, I made my way up the palace walls to my old bedroom.

My aunt waited inside, as though she'd guessed I'd come today, and I wondered if she snuck to my room daily for peace from the chaos of the palace.

"I need more," I whispered. "I read the book you gave me, but the text is old. It's over my head and there are many parts I don't understand."

Aunt Matzie pressed her lips together, the blood draining from her olive complexion as she shook her head slightly. "Nothing in there was helpful? What of the ancient magic? Surely some of it pertains?"

"If it does, I don't know how to use it, not against him. The sorcerers might know, but..." I shrugged.

Clasping her hands in her lap, she stared at the barren fireplace before relenting. "They store the old texts in the temple, but I don't like the idea of you going there. It's dangerous if they catch you."

"What about you? Can you go? Surely that's where you pulled that book from?"

Her eyes darted around the room as she shook her head. “I cannot go back. They caught me. Once.”

I recalled the cracking sound my uncle’s hand made as it slapped my face, and the feeling of my stomach cramping from his blows. Gingerly, I touched my belly, even though the bruise had healed. Yet, as I looked at my aunt, I realized she’d been privy to more abuse than I assumed.

Lifting her chin, she went on. “I have the children to think about, and if I’m caught talking to you… ”

She trailed off, but I understood.

Crossing my arms, I frowned. “But if we’re on the same side, why would they be angry?”

“No one trusts you,” she admitted. “They’d assume you had enlisted me to help you and we’d both be punished for interfering.”

I chewed on that for a moment, aware of the weight of her words. “Why haven’t you left?”

Aunt Matzie averted her eyes. “Where is there to go? I stay for the children.”

“But they are growing up here. Under this!” I gestured helplessly. “Once they are grown, they will just repeat the crimes of their ancestors and the cycle will continue.”

She jerked her chin up and rose. “That is why we have to stop the Piper. I’ll tell you where to go. In the temple, behind the curtain, is a series of doors.

The first one leads to the library, but they keep it locked."

My hand went to my chest, where the key Oren had given me lay against my skin. The key to unlock things that were sealed with magic. He wanted me to try it on the magic-thralls, but the idea of going back into the vault made me feel physically ill.

"I'll worry about the lock," I explained. "Where are the important papers likely to be kept?"

Aunt Matzie gave me directions and I memories her instructions. As I placed my hand on the door-knob, her soft words floated to my ears. "Don't get caught, Tanith."

As I slipped out and made my way down the halls —wondering what foul creatures Oren had summoned this time—another thought occurred to me. My aunt was a victim of this, a silent sufferer who had endured. Why? Had the unfortunate events of her life kept her cowed and submissive? Or was there something else I was unaware of that kept her passive?

The air of the palace was heavy with apprehension, and whispers from behind closed doors floated to my ears as I passed. Heart in my throat, I continued until a door opened. I flattened myself on the wall, hoping whoever was on the other side was a friend, not a foe, but when I saw Carter, my heart twisted.

His eyes lit up when he saw me, a reminder of how I'd taken advantage of his crush on me.

"Tanith, you're back." He frowned. "Why?"

"Not for long." Shaking my head, I squeezed his arm. "Carter, listen and listen carefully. Something terrible is going to happen in this city. You need to flee while there is still time."

"And go where, Tanith?" He grabbed my hand and pressed it between his. "We were supposed to rob the grave and run away together. Now we don't have any money."

I winced at the reminder of the night everything went wrong. "Money will not matter soon. The Piper will stop at nothing to get what he wants, even if he has to destroy everything and everyone. You've seen the plagues."

A shadow crossed Carter's face. "I have. He's dangerous. You need to get away from him."

"Don't worry about me, Carter, I have a plan. It's you and Kinder who need to get away safely."

He sighed. "And what will you do?"

"What I've always done. I'll survive."

Without waiting for an answer, I continued to the temple.

My shoulders tensed as I slipped through the side

door and the scent of burning flesh from a sacrifice filled my nostrils. The intense smell had almost a hypnotic effect. If I breathed too deeply, it felt as though I'd become a malleable version of myself, easily caught and controlled if I wasn't careful. Holding my sleeve over my nose, I held my breath as I crept toward the curtain.

The priests who prayed at the altar kept their backs toward me, unaware of my existence thanks to Oren's magic. But how long would that last? I'd been lucky once, twice even, but eventually my luck would run out, and I didn't want to imagine what they'd do if they caught me.

Slipping behind the curtain, I studied the rooms, my eyes drawn to the doorway that led down to the vault. My skin prickled with discomfort, aware of what went on far beneath me and how powerless I was to stop it. Despite my musings, no good ideas had come to me about what to do and how to prevent the destruction of Dowler.

The door to the library was locked, as expected, but I put the key in the lock and it opened without hesitation. The door gave a soft sigh as it swung open, and the perfume of paper and ink filled my nose. I breathed in, suddenly reminded of the halls I'd studied in when I was younger—the classroom, the scratch of a pen on paper, the rustle of turning pages.

Memories would only leave me trapped in inaction, so I closed the door, hoping I was alone. Anyone could have been hiding behind the rows of old books and towering shelves. I peeked around each one, my blood rising, then falling, when the empty rows revealed I was truly alone. The musty scent of parchment made my eyes water and gentle sighs floated to my ears, as though the books were alive and breathing. Magic dwelled here, just like in Oren's castle.

The bookcase in the back of the room had a hidden door on the second shelf, just as my aunt had promised. Inside was a stack of papers, and I unfolded them to reveal drawings, including the runes on the doors to the vault. There was also some prose, written in an old language I did not understand, and following it was a brief explanation of the rock within the vault that kept the Others from using their power. I held everything Oren needed to put a stop to this. My chest went tight in recognition of the power I held. Blackmail. All I had to do was think of how to use the knowledge to my advantage.

Stuffing the folded papers into my pocket, I started to make my way out of the library when the door opened and muffled voices swept through the room. I strained my ears, catching the end of their conversation. "He should make a deal with the Piper before it gets worse."

"Bah, they will never agree and you know why."

"Is revenge that important? I know I shouldn't speak of the past, but what if we simply gave the Piper what he wanted?"

"Are you a fool?" the second voice spat, louder than a whisper this time. "The magical system would collapse."

"True, but the system was created decades ago when the city was young and suffering from plague and famine. What if the city could sustain itself without magic?"

I slowly let out the breath I'd been holding as I considered that idea. This was the first reasonable solution to the problem. True, Dowler was wealthy. Originally, I assumed it came from trade, not magic, but I'd never asked. Suddenly interested, I strained to hear more.

"Surely a payoff would keep him happy. He's immortal, you know."

"Not quite."

"No, what do you mean? There's a way he can die?"

"Eventually he'll reach an old age and pass from this world, hundreds of years after our lifetime. But to best him now, we have to destroy something mortal he treasures, or trap his magic and render his flute useless."

"And you have ideas on how we might achieve such a disruption?"

"Correct."

"Does it involve his new wife?"

"No." The man snorted. "She's too new to be of value. I suspect he keeps her tied up in the castle for his own amusement, unaware that the Lord and Lady of Dowler do not care what becomes of her."

I bristled at the vivid image of my life as a prisoner, although it was true my uncle had done nothing to free me from the Piper.

"Then you design to trap his magic?"

"Aye, he's very careful, so we must create an enticing proposal."

The voices moved further into the room, and while I wanted to listen, I needed to leave before they found me. Creeping from shelf to shelf, I made my way to the entrance. The priests were nowhere in sight, and I opened the door and fled.

21. Tanith

The palace was oddly silent, with no sign of Oren's magic. A growing dread knotted in my belly as I hurried to my old bedroom. What had he summoned with his music this time?

Inside was empty, and—relieved to avoid my aunt's questions—I climbed out the window and sprinted across the courtyard to where Oren's devilish horse waited. Unable to shake the feeling of unease, I faced the palace. The towers glared down at me, as though they knew I was an intruder in a building that had never felt like home.

A sharp wind blew, marring the sunny day, and when I tilted my head back, ominous black clouds rolled over the mountain. A storm was brewing, a bad one from the looks of those clouds.

The sonorous notes of a flute sounded, and I

pulled my head back down as Oren strode toward me, surrounded by a halo of golden light. His flute was against his mouth and his fingers danced gracefully up and down the length of it. Despite my mixed feelings about him, he looked like an angel of death, and his dark beauty and magnificent power left me breathless and weak-kneed. I wasn't used to feeling helpless, but around him, I was out of my depth.

He broke off rather abruptly and held out his hand to me. It was cold when we touched, but he drew me to him, deep eyes skating over my face. The wind tugged at his red hair, blowing it straight back from his smooth brow.

He angled his head as though he would lean down and steal a kiss. I licked my lips in anticipation, tasting a hint of salt in the air. The moment stretched as he held me, and I waited, barely daring to breathe, aware of his allure. Instead of kissing me, he tossed me on the horse's back and mounted behind me. His warmth enveloped me even though his hands were still cold.

With a sharp command, he spurred the horse onward, and we bolted out of the gates as if the demons of hell were racing at our heels. Perhaps they were, for the wind howled behind us. I clung to the horse's mane, feeling as though, despite Oren holding me, the impending storm would blow us away.

The rich and pungent stench of fear clung to the city as we passed—the devil on his demon horse with his bride, who wasn't as reluctant as she should have been. Behind closed doors and windows, the people looked on, furious but helpless, cursing our names as we passed. My heart lurched at the thought of being so hated. All because of the Piper.

We slowed when we reached the forest. The wind wasn't as strong there, buffered by the trees. Pine and cedar replaced the odor of the city, and I consider the priests' words about the magic-thralls and trapping Oren's magic. I had to warn him, but I wondered about the years of his life, how much darkness he'd seen, how long he'd lived, and how many times someone he loved been cruelly taken from him.

The tale of the Piper came again to my mind, the false story told to the people to keep them in fear. How much of it was true? Would Oren explain the full story if I asked? Patting my pocket, I recalled I had leverage, although it seemed wrong to use it against him.

Mentally, I steeled myself for our conversation as we trotted into the courtyard, and a beast rose from the doorway. A scream of terror burst from my lips before I could stop it, and I tried to scoot back, but Oren did not budge.

Mouth open, I stared as a dog-like creature trotted toward us. It walked on four massive legs, covered in short, chocolate-brown fur. Its tail was a mere stump, but it wagged it nonetheless as though it were happy to see us. Yet I could not look away from its face. It was round and smashed in. Instead of skin, there was nothing but skeletal bone and eye sockets, black as night. A hell dog, a mutt of horrors. I lifted my legs higher, whimpering as Oren swung down behind me.

"Barnum, at last," he said. "I thought you were lost."

Barnum gave a sharp bark in response, and Oren grunted before turning back to me.

"Tanith, I'm taking Barnum to the barn. Would you like to come?"

"I'd rather stay in the castle while you deal with your hellish beasts," I snapped, my fear getting the better of me. The image of being ripped from limb to limb would not leave my mind.

To his credit, Oren held out his palm to Barnum. "Stay, old friend, I'll be right back."

I shuddered at his use of the word "friend," although I had to admit I had Pip, an ugly gargoyle as my confidant within the castle. Suddenly, I just wanted to be back in my room.

Oren escorted me to the door, shielding me from the hell dog with his body. I would have considered it chivalrous if I hadn't been shaking. It was only when we stepped inside and he shut the door that my fear subsided.

Holding my arm, Oren studied me, a frown making his brow pinch. "Are you going to be okay?"

"Yes, I'm just going upstairs," I reassured him.

He tilted his head as though he didn't believe me and added, "I'll return before supper."

After he left, I closed my eyes and took deep breaths to calm my panic. When I had been a schoolgirl in Solynn, I used to cut through an alley on my way home from school. Even though it had rotten trash and smelled foul, it shaved ten minutes off my walk. I had been in a hurry that day, and didn't see the stray dog until I'd stepped on its tail. It lunged, barking, teeth snapping. I'd screamed as it latched onto my leg and bit deep, shaking and wiggling. Fortunately, the bite had healed without leaving a scar, but ever since that day, wild dogs made me shiver.

That hell beast was the worst of them all with that skeletal face. I shuddered again, hoping I wouldn't have nightmares.

A loud thump made me jump, and I scurried to the window, pushing back the heavy curtain to peer outside. The wind blew so fiercely, the trees near the castle bent in half. A lump swelled in my throat as I recalled tales of terrible storms and winds so violent they ripped homes apart. Dry leaves and grass lifted off the ground, twirling in tiny circles, and then the rain came, pelting the earth as if giants poured buckets of water over the land. Had Oren summoned the weather gods? If so, they were furious.

The sky turned dusky, hiding the light of the sun, and tiny pebbles, round like eggs, rained down. They smacked into the ground with a thump, making tiny dents. I gawked. A storm of rain and hail. This was the next level of doom for Dowler.

Feeling sick, I backed away from the window, my mind reeling with what exactly I should do. Oren would stop at nothing to get what he wanted, and the more I helped him, the more I was bound to the fate of the city. I did not want death on my hands, but he'd made himself clear. Chewing my lip, I decided to speak with him again and beg him to see reason. Lord Faren and his sorcerers were the problem, but by punishing the city, Oren punished all the citizens, innocent or not. Something had to stop.

Frustrated, I marched to the stairs when a blur of black and blue flashed out of the corner of my eye. I spun to face it, eyes darting across the room somewhat hidden in shadows, window panes shaking from the storm. "Hello?" I called, listening to my voice echo. Speaking out loud made me feel better, although it wasn't like the gargoyles could answer.

In a hurry to be back in the somewhat safety of my shared room with Oren, I fled up the stairs, only pausing when a high-pitched, quavering voice floated to my ears. "Where are you going, pretty one? I just want to talk."

No. No, no, no. This couldn't be happening. Was I imagining things? Standing at the top of the stairs, I turned around, my eyes widening in alarm at the creature that stood at the bottom.

The word creature was rather unkind, for it was clear she was a woman dressed in rags that did nothing to hide her filth. I wondered if she'd taken over the castle while Oren slept. Cobwebs hung in her hair and a layer of dust surrounded her like a cloud of flour. Her skin was dotted with moles and other bumps, and her eyes were overly wide and red, as though she'd spent too much time in the dark.

She grinned at my shocked expression, revealing sharp teeth. Too sharp for my liking.

"What are you doing here?" I demanded, fingers going to my thigh where my knife was hidden.

"Same as you." She shrugged, causing her rags to

slip off one shoulder. “Looking for shelter from the storm.”

Pulling the knife free of its sheath, I lifted my chin. “The Piper shall return any moment, and I don’t believe he will be happy with you trespassing on his property.”

She giggled, actually giggled as though she were five-years-old instead of some ancient hag who should be dead.

I scowled.

“Oh, the Piper. You don’t seriously believe in his magic.”

“I’ve seen it with my own eyes,” I retorted, wondering why I was about to get into an argument with a hag when I wanted to be in my room. It was rather disconcerting that she was in the castle at all.

“Please.” The hag rolled her watery eyes. “He’s no match for me.”

And then, with surprising quickness, she bounded up the stairs and landed in front of me with an inhuman, feline leap.

I staggered back, frightened by her speed. Bringing my hand up, I pointed the knife at her. “Get away from me,” I spat.

“I enjoy a good hunt.” She took a step, closing the distance between us. “But it’s too late for that now. I’m rather hungry.”

Adrenaline rushed through me as I squeezed the knife to keep my fingers from shaking. It occurred to me that I should have asked Oren to teach me how to use it instead of trusting my instincts. The hag pounced, knocking my hand away.

My wrist struck the wall, and I dropped the knife as I fell, limbs flailing as I struggled to protect myself. Something hard stabbed my side. Arching my back, I screamed, fingers reaching for the weapon that wasn't there. I went numb as a haze came over me. Weakness surged through each limb, and the hag peered down at me, her curved fingernails patting my cheek. When she spoke, it sounded as though her voice came from a void. "That's better. Now. Time to eat."

Valiantly, I attempted to struggle, but whatever she'd done had paralyzed me. My chest tightened as though my breath was being stolen away, and I faded out of consciousness.

22. Oren

My thoughts drifted to Tanith as I stood under the awning of the barn, watching the bullets of silvery rock flatten the land. If anyone were out in the storm, they would return home bruised unless they sought shelter, but the goose egg sized hail wasn't big enough to kill.

Barnum sat a few feet away, gnawing on a bone that smelled a little too fresh. Hunks of bloody meat still clung to it, a bit of his latest kill he'd taken the time to drag along with him. I was used to such gruesomeness, but Tanith's fear had been raw and ripe, as if I'd set Barnum on her. He was rather fearsome to look at with his skull on the outside. He didn't belong in this world, but I'd only summoned him out of need. Now I reconsidered. Perhaps the hail was enough and Lord Faren would see reason.

"I need your pack to be nearby, ready for my summons," I told Barnum. "The city of Dowler has to be ripe with fear, ready to fall to my demands, but there should be no death, only fear."

Barnum lifted his ears, his dark eyes acknowledging my request as he chewed. I hoped his pack was still as big as it had been previously—a motley crew of half-starved canines with a thirst for blood and human flesh. They enjoyed the hunt, mainly the fear of their prey, and Tanith's reaction had been enlightening. The citizens of Dowler would revolt. Plague and fear could only last so long, and then they'd mentally break. But would they be strong enough to stand up to Lord Faren, or would they flee?

Bitter memories plagued me, and unable to shake them away, I decided to return to the castle. Tanith had news for me. I sensed her anticipation, and she'd returned earlier than I'd expected. With her help, this could be the turning point to end my quest for vengeance once and for all. Leaving Barnum to his bone, I stepped into the storm.

Wind and rain swirled around me, then paused as I lifted my hands, the halo of magic surrounding me blocking off the advances of the storm. It obeyed, for I was the one who had summoned it. The magic held until I reached the doors of the castle and slipped inside to peace.

An odd musk hung in the air and I sniffed, frowning at the scent. It smelled ancient, like moss and dried leaves. Like dead things lying in hibernation on the forest floor, waiting for the light to bring them hope and embed them into the cycle of renewal. What was it?

I strode to the stairs, the light muted in the storm's wake. Window panes shook, and the hail sounded like a clattering of jewels against the glass. It reminded me of a lifetime ago when I was a boy and crystals had rained from the heavens. The orphans and I had collected them for our masters, and often, fights had broken out in the wake of those heavenly storms, for those who brought back the most jewels had been rewarded, and those who brought back the least, punished. Once, a boy older and stronger than me stole my bucket of jewels, leaving me with a tiny pouch. I was flogged, then starved for three days as a reminder I needed to be stronger, faster, better. Only the best survived.

Pale torchlight flickered as I reached the top of the stairs, pausing at the red sheen that covered the floor. Bright red blood, only a few drops and yet.... I bent, rubbing it between my fingers and sniffed. The only person alive in the castle was Tanith. Correction. *Should* have only been Tanith. But I'd evaded my duty of finding the unwelcome guest who might have taken up residence during my slumber.

My shoulders tensed and a pounding began in the back of my skull as I followed the trail of blood until it ended rather abruptly in the middle of the hallway. Either Tanith had cut herself and staunched the flow of blood or—my mind leaped to the worst conclusion—she'd been taken. I sniffed the air again, that musty scent oh-so-familiar, yet I couldn't place it. I followed the scent as it turned sweet and sickly, up the spiral staircase, my frustration swelling with each floor.

I passed the attic level and moved higher to the towers. I'd never cared much for them. Towers were where terrible things happened. Kings locked up their wives and daughters. Dragons guarded them, and knights rode in search of honor, to defend or save those within. And then there was my haunted past and the binding. It sounded like a fable.

Once upon a time, an all-powerful sorceress took great delight in punishing knights who displeased her by binding them to a tower. The tower was cursed and so were they, until time rendered the curse void, or the knights were forced to break it. All the while, immortality taunted them with longevity, and the torture never ended.

At the top, the stairs spilled into a concave room —the opening shrouded by a black curtain. I stilled in awareness just outside, recognizing my foe. A witch, probably experienced in the art of dark magic. Tanith. How long had it been since she was taken?

Any minute, the witch would sense my magic and prepare. Lifting my flute, I moved quickly, lightly side-stepping through the curtain into her lair. It was gloomy, with tendrils of smoke curling around my ankles. Faded pale lights hung from the ceiling, obscured by more dark drapery. A fireplace took up one side of the wall, large enough for someone to stand comfortably inside. Over the flames, a caldron bubbled with boiling, green energy. There, in the middle of the room, was the altar, with white bones, raven feathers, and my wife—spread-eagle, utterly naked—while that wicked witch did her work.

My vision tunneled as white-hot fury rolled through me. I wished to conjure a sword to strike the witch through her rotten heart. This was the beginning of a transference ceremony, to take a soul and force it to enter a new shell. A new body. The witch wanted to take Tanith's form, and if I hadn't arrived before it began, Tanith's soul would be lost to me forever. Already, her body was covered with cuts, and blood leaked out across the altar, a sacrifice to the gods.

My anger burned, and I lifted the flute to my trembling lips, wanting to strike out instead of remaining calm. But the magic would not work if I couldn't control myself. The first notes shook but steadily grew stronger as I played, first creating a protective barrier around myself. But I wasn't fast enough. The witch spun, eyes wide, and snarled, her open mouth revealing fang-like teeth, not unlike Barnum's.

It was clear to see why she wished for a new body. Her hair was knotted and wild, skin pock-marked and covered with blemishes. Whether it was her original body or one she'd worn down, it was impossible to tell. Not only was she a witch who practiced dark magic, she was a body-snatcher—a survivor, perhaps even as old as me.

"Come to save your bride?" she cackled, fingers moving as she formed a ball of black magic out of strands of darkness.

I played louder, trying to control the song while blood roared in my ears. She hurled the ball of darkness against my half-formed barrier. It dissipated under the onslaught, and tendrils of black magic slammed into me, knocking the flute from my mouth and hurling me against the wall. Pain radiated up my spine, followed by an intense burning sensation. With a groan, I stamped my feet and pressed my lips against the flute again, playing despite the pain. She was old, strong, and in her lair. However, I was old too, even if slightly weakened from calling the storm. We were equals.

The notes responded to my coaxing and drifted around me to reform the magical barrier, creating layers to strengthen it as the witch readied her black magic again. This time, I walked forward and her magic shattered against my barrier, clinking like glass against stone. I played faster, my fingers flying up and down the neck of the flute. My notes went down to the floor and lifted the shards of black magic, one by one, and hurled them like darts back at the witch.

She was quick, but not quick enough, and a shrill wail tore out of her throat as her own magic sank beneath her skin. I was good at revenge, and my lips curved up in a cruel smile, breaking the notes, but only for a second as I launched my offense. Using my magic to pick up objects in the room and hurl them at her, I distracted her from creating more balls of magic. All the while, I crept closer to Tanith, and my barrier of magic expanded, filling the room.

The witch clawed at the barrier with her overly long fingernails, causing sparks and smoke to rise. But I'd had just enough time to seal it. My blood boiled hot, making my body tremble as I reached

Tanith, who lay slack and unmoving. The witch hadn't taken the time to tie her up, so sure she had been in her power.

The attraction between Tanith and me was mutual, but beyond that, I hadn't realized I actually cared for my wife. Falling in love brought both bliss and an earth-shattering pain. I didn't think I had it in me to love again, especially a mortal who I intended to set free the moment she helped me succeed. I didn't plan on thinking of her again, except for a faint memory of the taste of her lips.

But now, seeing her laid bare—unconscious and being stolen from me—brought an overwhelming sense of protectiveness. Tanith was mine. How dare the witch attempt to take her away. I protected what was mine, and the witch had triggered more than just my fury. What was happening to Tanith was the same thing that had happened to the magic-thralls. Only, I'd failed in my duty to save them from damnation. But somehow, Tanith was different too. Her blood on the crystal had awakened me, and the vows of our marriage had created deeper bonds than I intended. Stirrings began in my chest, a cutting truth edging through my rage. My ears rang, my blood roared hot in my veins, and my heartbeat doubled. What I felt was more than protectiveness.

I slammed down the treacherous thought before

it fully formed and focused on the witch, aware I was about to lose control. She hovered in front of the fire, chanting as magic swelled from her palm, growing into something terrible and tormented. Was she pulling spirits from the other side?

I played one last note, bright and clear, and held it a beat before dropping my trembling hands to my side. A grin of mirth covered the witch's face. She thought I was giving up. But I couldn't play anymore, not with the new sensations stirring in my chest and the fury that beat against my head like a drum.

Even since awakening, I'd held everything in—my failure, my helplessness, my hatred, my confusion of coming to back life after so many decades had passed. Everyone from my past was gone. The mortals dead. The Others gone, either by banishment, punishment, or to the beyond where I could not follow. The creatures I called back to myself were from the grave and even if I succeeded, I'd still be alone. Forgotten. Just as if I'd been buried alive. Tanith made me feel less alone, less forgotten. Although she stoked my ire, she also awakened feelings that had long lay dormant, feelings I didn't realize I had until the witch tried to take her from me.

To prevent myself from accidentally breaking my

flute, I tucked it into my belt. I balled up my fists, opened my mouth, and roared.

All my emotions bellowed out of me, a deep bass surging into a higher tenor. The golden barrier between the witch and me flickered for a moment, as if it would go out without the music to sustain it. Then everything in the room flew as a wind storm kicked up.

I roared as the curtains twisted in a circle and the walls shuttered. I roared as the fire fell flat and the witch flew black, arms and legs flailing. Her bottom landed in the pot and she shrieked from the heat. I roared as my magic billowed out, humming, until—just like me—it exploded.

A violent boom shook the very foundations of the tower. Spinning, I lifted Tanith off the altar and ran while the stones crumbled and shattered. I barely made it to the stairs before the ceiling caved in and collapsing rock thundered behind me. I ran as if the devil and a horde of demons were behind me. Ironic. I was called the Devil of Dowler, but the devil wouldn't call up arcane magic to save his wife.

23. Oren

Back in our room, I washed the blood from Tanith's skin. If she were awake, she'd curse me with her sharp tongue. I'd gladly take anything other than the limpness of her body, as though her spirit were floating far away. I bound her wounds, dressed her in a nightgown, and laid her on my bed. She looked as though she were merely sleeping, her glossy, black curls trailing down her shoulders. I propped her up with pillows and sat down beside her, aware I, too, was weary and filthy from the explosion. Occasional tremors still shook the castle, aftereffects of the collapse of the tower. Likely a pile of rubble to shift through, but nothing that couldn't wait.

Taking Tanith's limp hand, I turned it over and felt for her pulse. It was weak, barely there. I pressed her hand between my palms, conflict rising like a bitter seed. My mouth tasted sour, but I had to decide in a matter of moments. If I waited, the ebb of life would flow away and Tanith—and the potential of what we could be—would be lost forever. And she was young. She wanted to live, and my blindness to anything else other than revenge might have cost me something beautiful.

Releasing her, I stormed to my shelves and riffled through the clutter until I found my hunting knife. Placing a cup on the desk, I held my arm out, and without preamble, slit my wrist. Blood gushed out, a deep red, almost black. The cup was half full when I stopped, wrapping my wrist with a bandage. It soaked through, but I'd close the wound later.

Returning to Tanith's side, I lifted her head. "Tanith, if you can hear me, listen. Drink this to live. It's medicine, it will heal you."

Her lips parted as though she heard me, even though her soul was in the balance between life and death. Despite the terrible thing I was doing, it felt like an acknowledgement, a consent to life. She wouldn't want to die like that, stripped of herself and shamed in the witch's lair. I would give her back her decency, her boldness, her life, and in time, she might forgive me for what I'd done. What I'd given her.

I held the cup to her lips until the last drops of blood were gone. My fingers slipped down the smooth skin of her arm to her pulse and waited. I waited while my blood-soaked bandage dripped on the bed, and at last, I was rewarded.

Her pulse thrummed, stronger, firmer, and the tightness around her body relaxed. The magic was working and my shoulders sagged. I hurled the cup into the fireplace and tossed the knife in too, as though I could hide what I'd done.

"I need a fire." I called to Pip. Odd how I used the name Tanith had given him. The dragon-like creature appeared, no wagging tail, sensing the air of wrongness in the room.

A ball of fire lit up the wood, and lapped at the stains of blood. I pushed the fire poker into the middle of the flame and waited, the heat warming the cool iron.

The storm I'd called to force the hand of Lord Faren. But changing his mind seemed an elusive goal, the one accursed desire for revenge I returned to again and again.

To break the cycle of morose thoughts, I loosened my bloody bandage, dropped it into the fire, and pressed the hot poker against my wrist. I gritted my teeth against the pain, but it still brought me to my knees as the scent of burning flesh filled the room.

All the energy I'd poured into the hailstorm, fighting the witch, and saving Tanith consumed me. A haze of blackness glittered, intoxicating, beckoning me into its depths. With one last gasp of soured air, I gave in to the madness.

24. TANITH

I woke to warmth and light and the scent of cedar. It was peaceful with the snap and crackle of a fire, and the whoosh of a gentle breeze from the patio. The curtains billowed out, then lay still again. I smiled, wondering if I'd gone back in time and was in my parents' house. Any minute, they'd burst into my room, calling out my name. I'd embrace them tightly, breathing in the comforting scent of father's pipe tobacco and mother's flowery perfume. I'd whisper all the things I wanted to say—how much I loved them, how proud I was to be their daughter, and how sorry I was we hadn't had more time together.

Time. I blinked as the last fragments of that daydream faded, and I realized I wasn't in my parents' old house, my room at the palace, or even in the windowless room Oren had given me. My heart kicked as it all came rushing back. Stealing from the temple, the demented hell dog, and being attacked by the hag.

After she caught me, everything was a blur. I had fragmented memories of a knife slicing through my clothes and then my skin. A fire so hot I thought I'd roast alive and a chant in my head. I was going to die and yet, somehow, some way, I'd been saved.

Now, I lay in Oren's room. In his bed. My face flushed hot, and suddenly, I was aware of every fiber of my body as I turned to the other side of the bed. He lay beside me, propped up on one elbow, studying me. His expression was a mix of relief and hope, like coming out of a long winter hibernation to the warmth of a spring sun. His eyes shone with a mix of unspoken emotions and words stuck in my throat. It was clear that he had saved me, and a rush of gratefulness and something else I dared not dwell on simmered within me.

"Tanith." He brought my hand to his mouth. "Finally."

When his lips touched my skin, the newness of our situation caused a flutter in my stomach. Something had changed between us. I was suddenly aware of the sheerness of my nightgown, even though the covers were pulled up to my shoulders, and the bandages that covered my arms and legs. More than anything, I sensed his heat—his presence—making me crave his touch.

"What happened?" I whispered, my voice hoarse from disuse.

Pain rose behind his eyes, and his brow darkened. "It's over now. How do you feel?"

"Alive." I shrugged my shoulders, but no weakness troubled me. I was awake and I felt very much alive, with strength surging through my veins and—my stomach rumbled loudly—I was hungry. "How long was I asleep?"

"You've been sleeping for seven days. Healing. You must be famished."

"Seven?" My eyebrows shot up in alarm. "How?"

Oren slid out of bed, shirtless, I noted with a sharp intake of breath. My gaze lingered on his back, for right below his shoulder blades were twin scars, each one about the length of my hand. Curious.

He padded to the patio and returned with a tray of food. I sat, letting the covers slip around my waist, and decided not to worry about modesty. With Oren, everything was different. He had never leered at me like the palace guards, and when his gaze lingered on the swells of my breasts peeking above the neckline of my nightgown, I felt desired in the most delicious way. Let him look, let him be tempted.

He sat the tray in my lap and propped up the pillows behind me, fingers brushing my skin. I swallowed hard, unsure if I was hungrier for food, answers, or him. But the food won.

"Take it slow," Oren cautioned, sitting on the edge of the bed so that he faced me.

Obediently, I chewed while he watched. When he was satisfied I wouldn't gorge myself, he explained.

"A body-snatcher, an elder witch with dark magic, captured you. I believe she took up residence here while I was gone and saw our return as an opportunity to steal your body. She likely studied our movements to ensure you'd be alone in the castle and waited until her magic was strong enough to perform the ritual."

"But you defeated her." I breathed. Obviously, or else I would not be here.

He inclined his head. "I did, but not without consequence."

Instead of holding my gaze, he stared off at the fire, his side profile thoughtful, sad even. Or was it something else? I popped a grape into my mouth and chewed, the first hints of misgivings stirring. "Tell me." It was a plea, not a command.

Squaring his jaw, he faced me again. "A body-snatcher needs a mortal body to dwell in. The witch was dying and needed a new body, a younger one. I caught her in the middle of a transference ceremony which would have forced your soul out of your body and allowed hers to take your place."

The fruit tasted like ash in my mouth. "I didn't know that was possible."

"Anything is possible with magic," Oren confirmed. "We dueled and destroyed a tower. I did a thorough examination of the damage, and many sections of the castle are uninhabitable now."

"And my clothes?"

"Gone."

"Oh. Oren, I had… I found…"

He waved his hand, stopping me. "It doesn't matter anymore."

My heart kicked. "Surely you don't mean that your vendetta against Dowler is over?"

"No." His brows drew together. "That still stands, but I need to go about it in a different way, I see that now."

I almost held my breath. Was this an apology? Or as close to one as I would get from him? Yet his eyes kept sliding away.

"Oren, what is it you're not telling me?"

"Tanith, are you… glad that you're alive? If you had a choice, would you choose life?"

No longer hungry, I gripped the bed covers. What

was he saying? "Yes, of course. Life versus death, I'd choose life every time."

Running his fingers through his hair, Oren paused before responding, his words tumbling out of his mouth in a rush. "Well then, you need to know that when I healed you, I gave you a gift, and I'm not sure what repercussions it will have."

"What do you mean? Will you explain and stop talking in riddles?"

"I gave you my blood."

Dread made me first cold and then hot. What exactly did that mean? And then my mind flashed back to a conversation we'd had just over a week ago. "Does that mean I'm like you? Immortal?"

"I'm not sure," he admitted. "Life is in the blood and you were dying. I didn't have a choice. I did what I thought was right in the moment because, Tanith, I—I don't want to lose you."

And it was that admission that shook me. My jaw dropped as his amber gaze held mine, daring me to argue or look away. Oren. The Piper. This deathly attractive inhuman, my husband, had done something out of the fear of losing me. Even though I was a mere mortal, who had committed an unspeakable act by stealing from him, he wanted me.

For a full minute, we stared at each other, tension

mounting as all the spoken and unspoken words between us sank in. The realization was so powerful and impactful, a frenzy washed over me. Two years ago, my life had turned upside down, forcing me to the hellish city of Dowler, with all appearances of paradise hiding a grave secret. My uncle had seized my dowery while my aunt turned a blind eye to the mistreatment I had endured within the palace. Fearing my future would hold only darkness, I'd felt forced to take drastic action, only to find myself married to a monster. Except the fables had lied about him.

Oren was the Piper, yet his flute only sang death to those who opposed him. To me, he was a misunderstood terror, hellbent on destruction because circumstances forced him to take extreme action, just like my situation had. But now, my grip on my self-control was shattering, and this was all I could take. No more holding back, no more waiting, wondering, trying to escape his allure.

I smacked the tray of food off my lap, and it clattered on the floor. Oren's eyes widened in horror as I launched myself at him. His broad hands rested on my hips as he leaned back to study my face. "You're not … angry?"

"Angry?" I settled myself in his lap, wrapping my arms around his neck. "You did the right thing,

Oren. Never apologize for that because I want to live. I have so much to live for."

His relief was palpable, and his protective arms tightened around me. For just the briefest moment, his eyes searched mine for confirmation before he consumed me.

When his fevered lips touched mine, a fire spread through every fiber of my body, an inferno that burned as though he were pouring his passion, his need for connection, into me. I hadn't realized how lonely I was as my body awakened, as if this was the moment I'd come back from the dead for. A lightness filled my chest and my breathing became heady and fast, pants of desire between frenzied kisses as his fingers twisted through my hair, pulling me closer. He'd kissed me before, but today, his kisses were a hundred times more potent and powerful and intoxicating.

Weak-kneed and dizzy, I let desire burn through me as I straddled him, the hem of my gown slipping up my legs. His muscled chest brushed against my breasts, making my nipples peak and ache. Teeth pinched my lips and his hips rolled against mine, while one hand came down to test the firmness of my buttocks. A groan rolled out of my mouth, answered by one of his own. His hand slid up my thigh, under my nightdress, and my breath came faster.

Eyes closed, I gave in to his heated caresses, wanting him, needing him as desperately as I needed air to breathe. My thoughts were twisted and muddled, for something had happened, something had changed, and my lust for him had morphed into something else. Something I dared not name.

Oren's mouth was all-consuming, and he trailed fervent kisses down my neck. My nightgown slipped down one shoulder, and he pressed gentle kisses against my bare skin, his pace slowing to a calm reverence as he held me. When he pulled back and hooked a finger under my chin, a wetness shone in his eyes, and he studied me as though I were some rare treasure he'd just unearthed.

"You," he murmured, his face drawn, serious. "You enchant me."

My hands rested on his chest, his racing heart pumping against my palm. Tilting my head, my gaze dragged from his eyes to his lips. Oh, heavens, if he kissed me like that again, I would not be able to resist. "How? When it is you who saved me?"

His jaw tightened. "Yes, well, the effects of that are yet to be determined."

The thread of unease that passed through me

could not quench my desire. "What is it you think will happen?"

"It is better not to speculate." When I opened my mouth, he shook his head. "Don't argue, Tanith, it is I who owe you the apology."

I narrowed my eyes at him. Ever since I'd met him, he'd lectured me on the consequences of my actions. But he plunged onward, with words I did not expect. "Ever since you awakened me, I've been focused on the magic-thralls and their freedom because they are like me, the only family I have. Every action I've taken with you has been for selfish reasons. I've left you alone far too often, and did not take steps to ensure your safety here. I knew something lurked in the castle, but I never imagined it would be a body-snatcher."

I wiggled in his arms, for I still straddled him and the heat of his body crept through to my core. Sliding my hands up his biceps to his shoulders, I held his gaze. "What happened is done and over. It's in the past now. The best we can do is move forward and remain honest with each other. It is unfortunate but …" With a shrug, I trailed off.

Dipping his head, he kissed my shoulder and when he spoke, it was so softly, I almost missed it. "True, but it made me realize how important you are."

Sucking in a deep breath, I blurted out the question before I lost my courage. "Oren, what changed between us?"

He went still. Both arms tightened around my waist.

"I made a choice," he admitted, before facing me. "Tanith, it was you, always you, even though you woke me. I admit, I wanted you to be my bride, and yes, my power protects you, but ... there are others ways. This was the easiest way to make you mine, and I protect what is mine. No one will take what is mine away, unless I will it."

His eyes went hard, and a possessiveness laced his tone. His silken, red hair brushed against my fingers and I studied him, not sure I understood. Was it love? Possession? Something darker? And with a jolt, I recalled the hushed conversation of the priests. They wanted to take something mortal from the Piper to punish him, and if it were me ... what did that mean for us?

"You're thinking." He loosened his hold on me. "Don't overthink it, you just woke up."

"I know." I bit my lip. "I was simply wondering what happens now? To Dowler? The runes I found were in the clothes I was wearing when the witch took me. But surely you still have a plan?"

"Yes, I have a plan, but you should rest. Regain your full strength and then we shall strike again."

"And what shall we do about these feelings between us?"

"I know what you think, Tanith, but until we know for sure what has happened to you, we should not consummate our marriage."

I bit back my retort, unable to deny that his words hurt me. Was it wrong of me to desire my devastatingly dark, yet beautiful, inhuman husband?

The glow of happiness faded for he'd cast an invisible barrier between us. Although his eyes beseeched me not to be angry with him, a veil of clarity had been drawn over our conversation, forcing a rift between us.

"Come." He dropped his arms. "I'll draw you a bath, and then if you're up to it, I'll show you the ruined tower."

I nodded, giving in to him while wishing that things were somehow, someway, different.

25. Tanith

Lavender and eucalyptus soaked through my skin as I lay in the tub, letting the warm waters relax me. Even though I remembered little of what had happened to me, it was soothing to relax and take off my bandages. Oren had done his work as a healer well, for the knife wounds on my skin had already knitted back together, leaving only faint scars. It was too early to tell if they'd fade completely or whether I'd carry the signs of the encounter on my skin forever.

I weighed Oren's words as I washed. He remained in the room, telling me to call if I had need of him. I deliberated over the fact that he'd given me his blood. *His blood.* I wanted books; I wanted to read and study and find out what that might mean. He claimed to be a healer, and yet, he'd used the magic in his blood to ensure my soul stayed. What repercussions would it have?

Closing my eyes, I sank under the water, listening to my rapid heartbeat. Since awakening, my desire for him had increased. But perhaps that was only a false sensation. Maybe it was his blood calling out to him, wanting to return, and I was simply a vessel. Resurfacing, I shook my head hard to clear the confusion that lurked in my mind like cobwebs in the high ceilings of the castle.

I had to focus on what I wanted and my future. This incident with Oren was but a blip in my life before I returned to Solynn, where body-snatchers did not dwell in the shadows, music did not summon creatures, and inhumans did not exist.

When I got out of the tub and toweled off, there were tears on my face, and I did not understand why.

Later that afternoon, after plying me with more food and drink, Oren escorted me through the castle. I stiffened when we reached the front doors, thinking of the hell dog, but outside, the summer sun was warm and the air smelled like fresh flowers. Signs of the storm had vanished. The breeze was gentle, and no skull creatures threatened to terrify me. Sweet bird song hovered in the distance, and Oren held me close as we walked.

We circled the castle to where half of the

sprawling building had been completely and utterly destroyed. Stones had crumbled into dust, and a pile of rubble rose three times as tall as me. Tiny balls of dust kicked up in the wind, and from the ruins wafted a faint scent of sulfur.

"This?" I breathed. "All this?"

"The magic was destructive," Oren explained. "I searched as much as I dared, but I hope nothing survived that."

I nodded, closing my eyes briefly as a memory of intense pain made me shudder. "I think I've seen enough."

Oren—attuned to the state of my emotions—led me away. "While you were healing, I walked through the entire castle to secure it with wards against evil. The gargoyles helped wall up the entrances to the damaged part of the castle, but I found something I did not expect."

"And what was that?"

"You may not know this, but underneath the castle is a labyrinth of tunnels."

My mind flashed back to the vault, to the dark things crawling underground, blood and torture, and magnificent creatures, bound by foul magic. My fingers tightened around his arm. "Where do they lead to?"

"Some connect to the graveyard, that's how I initially brought you to the castle."

Ah, that explained the night we met, and how quickly he'd moved me.

"One tunnel leads to the palace, although I had that entrance blocked a long time ago."

I raised my eyebrows, studying his chiseled face. "Why? What's the point of connecting this castle to the palace when, according to past legends, no one wanted to have anything to do with you?"

His lips thinned as he tilted his head and gave me a wry look. "There are many tales about me, aren't there? What do they say?"

"Those tales are dark because they don't reflect the truth of your character. They only highlight your dark side, and even that has been embellished."

"Tell me," Oren whispered, the song in his tone too impossible to ignore.

"You won't like it," I warned him.

He shrugged. "It's been a long time since I cared about someone's opinion of me."

I sighed and took a deep breath, repeating the tale Uropa had first told me, followed by the whispers that echoed in the palace. "Many say you saved Dowler with your flute, and when you weren't rewarded for your actions, you turned the woods into a snare. Children were warned to stay away or they might be lured to their deaths by the Piper's song, lured by the dusk.

"The tales go so far as to claim that the Piper steals souls and hearts, making people nothing more than puppets, eager to obey, even if it meant lifting a knife and slitting their own throats. But beyond mind control, when people went into the forest, they disappeared and no one has an explanation for that. Is it true though? Did all that happen long ago? You saved the city from plague and famine, and they cast you out?"

Oren snorted when I finished. "They've confused me with the King of Hearts."

I raised an eyebrow. "Who's the King of Hearts?"

"A friend from before. We grew up together." Oren went quiet, lost in thought before he shook himself. "In the past, Dowler was my home."

My heart pounded as my curiosity spiked. "What do you mean your home?"

"I was sent here to be the protector of Dowler, to guard its boundaries, protect it from wild creatures and raiders who would come to plunder the new settlement. This castle, which overlooks the city, was my home, but as the city grew, the citizens demanded a leader. A lord was chosen to rule, and because he was mortal, the people trusted him more. The city continued to grow, and the lord had a palace built, and then a temple. To spite me, I imagine. I built the tunnels and connected them to the palace to monitor him, but eventually, the people learned how to protect themselves and did not see a need for me anymore."

This was not the story I expected. "What about the magic-thralls?"

"They were guardians, honored as elders, who walked among the people and taught them the way of the gods. But the guardians trusted too easily, and the people—jealous of their immortality and magic—took advantage. They learned to control magic, and instead of relying on the guardians, betrayed and enslaved them, using their own magic against them."

A memory of what I'd seen in the vault made my chest go tight.

"Certain crystals weaken the physical bodies of the thralls, allowing the sorcerers to drain their magic and use it to sustain the city. It's a slow, painful process, brought about by bleeding the thralls. Their blood runs blue and once they are drained, I imagine they are allowed to rest and regain their strength before the cycle begins again. It wouldn't surprise me if sometimes the sorcerers drink their blood to strengthen their own magic. I cannot imagine the fouls things that take place in the vault, but it needs to end."

My mind reeled with the truth, and the dark fable about the Piper, twisted to make the citizens fear the immortal who was once their savior. "What about you? How did you escape imprisonment?"

"I wasn't there when they rounded up the guardians and locked them in the vault because the Lord of Dowler was smart and assumed I'd notice a mass exodus. Instead, he took the guardians, little by little, and by the time I realized he had betrayed us, it was too late. I fought to free them by raining down destruction on my land, my kingdom, but the Lord of Dowler was just as stubborn then as he is now, full of a lust for power and greed for wealth.

"Worst of all, he and his sorcerers were prepared for my anger, and they would not relent because they had magic of their own. Some of the citizens were on my side, and they came to my castle to help, but without magic, they could do nothing. Eventually, I sent them away through the tunnels that led to escape. I gave Dowler everything, I brought the city into existence, and I knew the day would come when they did not need me anymore. But I did not expect them to take the guardians and abuse them. That is unforgiveable."

Oh. The threads of the story fit perfectly. Those who had disappeared in the woods, the rot in the palace, the stubbornness of my uncle. But I had one more question and desperately needed an answer. "When the guardians are free, what will happen?"

"I will send them home, for the world does not deserve their gifts. Magic was given and abused, and so it must be stripped from this world, for those with power will always abuse and seek to use magic for evil deeds. Tales claim I have no heart and my focus is revenge, and it is true. I hold great power, and I will not stop. I will not relent until they are free. You should know this about me. If what is mine is taken, I will take it back and wreak havoc on those who seek to harm me and my people."

Jealous. Relentless. Just like he'd been for me against the witch. I considered my aunt, my young cousins, and my fearsome uncle. The entire city would suffer the consequences of the past, but Oren was right. The magic-thralls had to be set free, and perhaps Dowler could rebuild. So far, I'd been playing along, playing his game, but as I stared up at my broad-shouldered husband, determination making his face hard, I decided once and for all to help him.

"Oren." I squeezed his arm. "I'm on your side."

His amber eyes bored into mine. "I hope you mean that."

And a chill went down my spine, cooling the warmth that had been spreading between us.

26. Tanith

"Tanith, come to bed."

The low timbre in Oren's voice sent shivers of liquid desire dancing in my loins. I stood in the doorway of my adjoining room and glanced over my shoulder at him. He sat on the bed, shirtless, a book in his hand, red hair flowing about his shoulders. Candlelight flickered, hiding his toned body.

For the past week, a peace lingered between us, a sort of stalemate as though the games afoot had paused and we were in a truce before the final battle began. We ate on the balcony, enjoying the warmth of the summer sun while Oren sewed me new clothes or traced runes. We swapped stories about the past. He told me how the wounded creatures of the forest were drawn to him. He'd fixed broken wings and legs, sewn torn skin and sheltered them in the barn until all forest creatures became his friends. That's why they came when his flute summoned them.

His stories were a peek into a gentler, softer side of him, a side that cared about something other than revenge and devastation. My heart skipped when I looked at him, so I kept my eyes focused on his work, the peppermint tea, Pip's wagging tail, anything other than Oren's perfect face and that new heat in his eyes that made my breath come short and fast.

When he asked me questions about my past, I told him about Solynn, the death of my parents, and how I came here to grieve, not knowing the darkness that crept through Dowler like rot. He listened intently, and the burdens of my past felt lighter and less wearisome after I'd shared with him.

Still, what had happened cast a cloud of allure over us. I desired him with a need that burned like an unquenchable fire. But his words about immortality rose like a barrier between us, making me second guess my craving. Was it his blood that made me burn? And if I had his blood, was I immortal too? Already a new strength surged through my body, and I wondered, when offered the prospect of eternal life, who would refuse? But the truth of it meant long years—endless, lonely years, some good, others bad. Look what eternal life had done to him. Would I be willing to risk it?

"To your bed?" I clarified, raising an eyebrow, letting my hesitation hang between us. I'd completely healed, even my scars had faded. There was no need to keep sleeping in Oren's bed like a patient.

"Why not? It's where you want to be."

"Is it where you want me to be?"

Closing the book, he crossed his arms, daring me to argue with him. "It is."

I did not move. "What are you going to do? Watch me while I sleep?"

"No, is it wrong of me to want my wife in my bed? To sleep side by side and feel a flicker of normality, like we are two lovers and not … this." He gestured impatiently as though that would give me an idea of what he meant.

"We aren't pretending," I filled in for him, a hole of emptiness, want, and despair growing in my heart. "I don't know if I can."

A lump swelled in my throat, almost choking me, longing for that normality. If my parents were still alive, I'd be in the city, married to a kind boy that eventually I'd love, but nothing like what Oren offered. His passion was hot, then cold, and when I closed my eyes, I felt his burning kisses sear my lips. It was intense, dangerous, and the truth was, I'd never felt more alive than when in his arms. This tantalizing dance of can and cannot would drive me mad. I sensed Oren carried his own demons on his shoulders that he was slowly showing me, little by little, allowing me a glimpse of what he'd lost through the years of his life.

I must have considered for too long, for Oren tossed back the covers and rolled out of bed with a grunt. He strode toward me and gathered me in his arms before I could protest.

"Come to bed, my lovely wife," he commanded, luring me with his tenor tones. "Come and pretend, just for tonight, that nothing exists except you and I. We have no cares, no worries, no plans. It's just us."

Instead of protesting, I leaned into his embrace, wrapping my arms around his neck. He lifted me as though I weighed nothing and carried me to his bed. We sank into the plush mattress and he released me, only to blow out the candle and cover us with the heavy blankets. I closed my eyes, my cheek pressed against his warm chest, listening to the steady thump of his heart.

Moments passed. My body relaxed and my mind drifted away. Somewhere between the edges of sleep and wakefulness, Oren's arms tightened around me and his mouth moved, a whisper I wasn't sure I heard correctly. "I need you, Tanith."

Those three words were all it took, as though he'd said "I love you." It had been so long, too long since I'd been held, and this pretending, this semblance of a marriage, was not enough. I needed more. Despite the risk and the edges of darkness that crept around my shaky future, I wanted to be bold and hold on to something real. Regrets and hesitations be damned.

Pushing him flat on his back, I straddled him, tossing my nightgown over my head. It landed with a whisper on the floor as I clamped my thighs around his hips, rubbing against his hardness. "I don't want to think about consequences," I whispered, emboldened by his sharp intake of breath. "I just want you."

I half expected him to push me away, but the enchantment of the night held him in its grip too. With a growl in his throat, he sat up, fingers catching in my hair, his lips like a brand as he kissed me. I opened my mouth and our tongues twisted in a dance of desire. Closing my eyes, I let the sensations of his touch take over. His hand on my hip moved to the small of my back, anchoring me to him, while his other hand came around to my chest, cupping my breast gently, tenderly.

Fissures of desire shot through my core, and I

moved my hips, grinding against him, wordlessly telling him I was willing, wet, ready. Oren broke the kiss, his lips touching the corner of my mouth as he worked his way down. I threw my head back and arched my back until my chest was level with his face. Panting, I begged. “Don’t stop.”

“I don’t intend to, my love,” he said, indulging in this pretense. Tonight, we were lovers.

Cupping my breast, he rolled the nipple between two fingers, making the bud harden until it hurt. The space between my legs ached, longing to be filled, to be taken. I gasped and shuddered as his tongue lashed first one nipple and then the other, sending shivers of delight up my spine. When at last he took one in his mouth, a mewl burst from my lips until he bit down. I squeaked and my eyes flew open. I started to sit up, but he slapped my bottom, a teasing tap before his fingers dipped to explore deeper.

No one had ever touched me there and my cheeks flushed. Pulling back, he lifted my other breast to his mouth. Breathless, I squirmed, overwhelmed by the sensation of his hardness against me, protected by a barrier of clothing. Even though he held me tightly, I managed to reach down and tug at his trousers, wiggling my fingers inside. When my hand touched his cock, he went rigid, then thrust, a groan coming from his core. I knew then what power I had. I squeezed and was rewarded with another groan. Had no one touched him like this? Had no one loved him?

"Tanith," he breathed, his head sinking down, pressing against my shoulder. "Don't stop, that feels like …" He trailed off and something like a frenzy overcame him.

He rolled, lifting me with one arm and placing me on my back. A moment later, his trousers hit the floor, and he planted himself between my legs, rubbing himself against my wetness. Shamelessly, I spread my legs and reached for him, one hand splayed against his chest as he slid into me. Oh, it was perfect as he filled me, and my body clamped around him as if we were made for each other.

Waves of pleasure rocked through me and I cried out, trembling as he held me steady. He waited a beat too long, and I rocked my hips up, silently telling him to proceed. Slowly, he pulled out of me, savoring the moment, and then thrust back. Hard. I arched into him as another bloom of pleasure spread through my body. He caught one of my hands and held it to his lips, kissing my palm and then my wrist before pressing my hand to his heart.

And that gesture—so tiny and seemingly insignificant—was what broke me. He didn't have to kiss me, didn't have to be tender and loving. Yet, the fact that he would kiss me as though we weren't simply using each other for pleasure made me feel wanted.

Wanted for more than my young and supple body, or that fact that I'd made a mistake and stumbled into his lair, making myself his. Yes, he was my husband, but our sham of a marriage had been for protection and convenience. Now, his actions spoke more than his words. I was precious to him. He chose to love me, crave me, protect me, and keep me alive. I spoke his name out loud. "Oren. Kiss me."

"Anything," he responded, his voice hoarse as he gathered me in his arms.

My breasts pressed against his chest, the skin-to-skin contact setting me aflame as he met my eager lips. Each kiss intensified the sensations, and even when stars danced around my head, I could not get enough. We moved together, taking and giving pleasure. With each thrust, my pleasure heightened, growing and coiling until I could not tell where I began and he ended. We were one, moving in sync, and I did not know whether it was real or magic. A cold realization came over me that in the past, when I'd been with others, it had been playing around, nothing compared to making love like this.

I climaxed hard, and he held me as I cried out, spasming in his embrace. When at last I stopped shaking, he turned me over on my hands and knees, kissing my shoulders, my back, my neck, his broad hands squeezing my breasts as he took me again. Another orgasm rolled through me, stronger than the last, making my toes curl. I screamed into a pillow even though there was no one to hear me. He slipped out of me as my body went limp and pressed heated kisses down my back to my bottom. Spreading my legs to kiss me there, his tongue tickled my wet slit, making me mewl with contentment.

"I'm not done with you yet," he whispered.

I trembled under his touch. For what more could he possibly give me? I was thoroughly spent. But I was wrong as he rolled onto his back, pulling me on top of him. Sinking into his embrace, I placed one hand on the side of his face, his silky hair brushing my skin. He smelled woodsy and clean, intoxicating, compelling and even though I felt sated, my hips rolled against his hardness again.

Pressing my lips to the hollow of his neck, I tasted him, and then bit down, delighting at the growls of pleasure I elicited from his lips. His pulse raced under my caress, making me aware of my power over him. This wasn't one-sided at all. My actions could drive him as wild as he drove me. His hand tightened around my bottom and then slapped, kneading and lifting, until I sat up.

Reaching down, I guided him up and into me, feeling his hardness pulse and then we were one again. But this time, I controlled the rhythm, guiding us like a song to the crescendo. Hands on his shoulders, the tips of my breasts grazing the hard pecks of his chest, I rode him, hard and fast. He held onto my hips, occasionally bringing a hand up to cup my swinging breasts until he went rigid, clasping me to his chest. He was still hard when he pulled out of me, and although my legs ached, I missed his fullness.

Shuddering, I rolled off him and lay flat on my back, chest heaving. Still, he reached for me, fingertips dancing down my arm, my leg. "Oren." I moaned, turning my face toward his because I was both exhausted and didn't want the night to end. I felt whole, complete, wanted. His teeth nipped at my flesh, arms slipping around my body, and he nuzzled closer, pulling me into his arms. Devils be damned, this was what I wanted. A love as true and passionate as this.

27. Tanith

When I woke, I quickly closed my eyes against the daylight, my dreams blissful, my sleep deep and restful. I felt reborn, but I didn't want to open my eyes, to face a day where Oren wasn't my lover. While last night held no regrets for me, I still recalled his attitude against making love, and the idea that he might give me an accidental gift of eternal life. The wrongs done to him had shaped his life, forcing him to impose his restrictive attitude on me and yet ... what if?

I let the idea dangle and could find no harm in it. Oren was powerful enough to control the magic of the flute but with it had come enemies. If I helped him gain revenge, what would be left to fill the empty space where his anger resided? Would he be able to fill it with love?

"I know you're awake." His words brushed against my skin like velvet.

My eyes flew open as I turned my head, his amber gaze so close, so heated. Despite myself, my eyes fell to the full lips I'd spent so much time kissing last night. Yet the urge to taste him again swelled within me. "Has no one loved you?"

"Not in a long time, a very long time," he answered, his voice tinged with regret.

"Because you won't let anyone in." I told him, placing my hand on his heart.

"Loving me is dangerous."

"But a life without love, so full of anger and regret and revenge, is no way to live."

He arched an eyebrow. "Are you judging me?"

"All I'm saying is that you don't have to push everyone away."

His fingers tiptoed down my arm to my belly, tracing my curves as though he could memorize them by touch. "I'm not pushing you away."

I examined his face for the truth, wanting to believe, yet wanting an excuse. "But you did, and you might if … "

"If what?" Darkness swirled in his gaze, and his eyes held mine, daring me to speak the forbidden words.

"If you discover that I'm like you."

He closed his eyes and turned his head, blowing out a frustrated breath. When he faced me again, that sense of remorse I'd feared made his mouth slope downward. "It's too late for that. We've consummated our marriage, which leaves us eternally bound, eternally cursed."

"Cursed?" Fear snaked through my body along with a warning. I'd known what I was walking into the moment I decided to steal from the dead. But cursed by the Devil of Dowler was almost too much to bear.

His lip curled. "Cursed, if you would call it that. Bound by desire and lust and fate until one of us dies, or is killed. Morbid, I know, but I shall always desire you, even when your heart grows cold, and that is my curse."

I punched his arm lightly. "That's not a curse. Those are feelings."

"Yes, and nothing I do is ever done halfway."

I'd noticed that about him in his intensity and fever for freeing the magic-thralls, ensuring I paid for stealing, owning the consequences of my actions, and then, last night, in making love. But cursed? No, he was just trying to frighten me. Placing my palm against his cheek, I brushed my thumb over his lips. He responded by turning his head and kissing my hand, sending tingles up my arm.

"You don't frighten me and I don't believe we are cursed." I told him. "If I've learned anything from you, it's that we have power over our desires. What you want comes into fruition. It's only a matter of time, especially if your will is strong enough. You could have let the witch kill me, but you destroyed her, taking down part of the castle with her. I've seen you fight to free the magic-thralls, and now I see that you have been giving Lord Faren a chance to do the right thing. But when the time comes, you will force his hand, and you will not relent because your magic is strong. It surges within you, begging to be let out to cause chaos, but you are measured and calm, in control, and you will remain that way."

"Will I? I took you against my better judgement. I healed you out of impulse, without weighing the costs. But you are right in one regard. I have stayed my hand and brought only terror to Dowler. But Lord Faren will not listen, will not relent unless true darkness comes to his household. Even if the city burns, he will not free the magic-thralls, so he has forced my hand. I will bring pain, personal pain to his household, and he will give in to my demands. But I dislike the sound of his name on your lips, nor do I want to discuss the fate of Dowler. Such darkness should be banished from our bed."

I made a move to rise, but he held me down with

a gentle pressure. Allowing him to keep me in bed, I asked. "When do we return to the city? I need to prepare."

"Tomorrow, as soon as the sun rises. But our original plan will have to be adapted because we don't have the time to unravel the secrets of priests and sorcerers. But later, I do not want to talk about it now."

"What do you want to do then?" I asked.

"Spread your thighs and I will show you."

My stomach fluttered at the idea of being taken again and so quickly. He knew what he did to me as I opened my legs and lifted my knees, showing him how wet and ready I was for him. And as he took me, again and again, turning me to different positions, I wondered if, indeed, it was a curse and not a blessing. When the time came, when the deal of our bargain had been met, would I be willing to leave all this darkness and lust behind and return to Solynn to start anew? How could I go on when this was the apex of life? I was married, taken, wanted, and this wasn't where I belonged. But it could be.

28. Tanith

To my chagrin, the next time we left the castle—riding on that terrible horse—a pack of skull-faced dogs followed behind us, their pants loud even above the thunder of hooves. The city appeared like a wilted leaf and the damage done by the hail was plain to see. Shops had holes in their roofs, crops had been flattened, some homes were only half standing. The pristine cobblestone road was missing stones, pockets of dirt cropping up. A staleness hung over the city. I glimpsed shadows in windows and imagined glares full of hate. A surge of mixed feelings rushed through me, for our coming was an omen of doom. I hoped those who were wise enough would pack up their goods and leave, for even when the scourge of Oren's revenge finished sweeping the city, I wasn't sure how much would be left.

We galloped into the courtyard, and Oren waved his hands to the hell dogs as we dismounted, a gesture I assumed meant for them to wait. They backed away, but not far enough, for I still shivered as Oren escorted me into the hall.

Lord Faren stood waiting with his sorcerers, as though they had known we were coming. For once, I did not slip away to spy, and I wondered what my aunt would think of my silence and the two weeks that had passed since we'd come.

We stepped across the threshold and paused. Oren, with his hand on the small of my back, drew himself up to his full height and addressed Lord Faren. "I've returned to hear your verdict. Will you let the magic-thralls go free?"

Lord Faren's deep voice boomed across the hall. "We've given your request consideration and have a compromise."

"Speak."

"We will give you the mine and you will leave us alone. Once you have proven you can do so, we will consider letting the thralls go free."

Oren spat at Lord Faren's feet. The vehemence in his action stabbing through me like a knife. I felt his anger boiling in my blood.

"You think something like a mine will appease me? It is the magic-thralls' freedom, or I shall rain down devastation on this land like you've never seen before. I will take everything precious you hold dear, and you will rue the day you did not give in to my demands. You've had decades to plot and plan your rise to glory, but you have abused the gifts given to you and used stolen magic for foul deeds. You've gotten away with it, but now the time has come for retribution and you will not survive long past this day. I shall return in three days, and I hope you'll have changed your mind."

We rode back in silence, although the barking and braying of those fearsome dogs echoed through the city. At one point, I heard terrified screams, and I wondered if someone was being bitten, limbs torn apart, even though Oren had promised the dogs would not touch or harm anyone. They were there to inspire fear, and I agreed that looking at them was enough. They barked, chased, and growled. Even astride Oren's horse—his hand pressed firmly to my belly—I could sense the fear of Dowler filling the air with its bitter octane.

We reached a hillock overlooking the city, and Oren stopped the horse before leaping down. I made a move to join him, but he held me still by placing his hand on my thigh. The heat of his touch was a reminder of the one day and two nights we'd spent in a frenzy of passion. Whatever had arisen between us was still there, leaving me wanting to run my fingers through his silken hair and wipe that murderous look off his face. Maybe it was the gift of his blood that had blurred the lines, for I couldn't tell where my plans and goals began and his ended. My thoughts revolved around him and his desires.

"Stay, I need to think," he said gently.

"About?" I prodded.

"How to enact my plan without hurting innocents, as you wish."

I bit my lower lip, surprised he'd listened to me in my boldness and anger, telling him his plagues affected more than the palace. "Do you want to talk through your plan?"

His eyes smiled at me, grateful, but his face remained hard. "No. Go back to the castle. I'll come shortly."

I'd heard those words before and the hope bubbling in my heart died. "Is that wise, considering what happened the last time?"

A muscle in his cheek jumped, and he tightened his jaw. "Or go to the barn. The hounds will not return today. Take solace in the comfort of animals and lock yourself in my workshop if you must."

I nodded, still staring at him, a whisper of unease beading under my skin. "You trust me not to run away?"

He studied me for a beat, drawing out the silence between us, and then lifted my hand and kissed my wrist. "Do you love me?"

My heart kicked under the spell of those words, a question I could not answer. Yet the way he looked at me, his soul rising in his amber eyes, told me more than words or actions ever could. Questions shattered like glass dashed upon rocks, but one thought stood out clearly. This was my chance to run even though I felt torn. But without money, I wouldn't get far and part of me wanted to find out what would happen to Dowler and Oren. I sensed he was close to achieving what he wanted, which would mean the end of him and me. I'd been little help to him, and even when I'd found something, I'd failed to deliver it because of that witch. Now, he sent me away because all along he'd had the strength to ruin Dowler.

"I …" My breath whispered and froze on the words, unable to go any further.

"I must earn your trust, I know that, but first, I must follow this through to whatever end. I cannot dwell here while the magic-thralls live in an endless cycle of torture, being drained of their magic, revived, and then put through the cycles again. This has to end, and I will send a sign that will let Lord Faren know that this time, I mean it. I will stop at nothing. So go, Tanith, don't watch me do this."

He slapped the horse's rump, and I pressed my lips together to keep my teeth from jarring. Curling my fingers into the horse's mane, I glanced back over my shoulder, but Oren wasn't watching me. He stared off at Dowler, looking over the city sloping beneath the hill and rising to the apex of the mountain where the palace loomed. A coldness passed over me as though I were watching the end, and a sense of finality hung in the air.

Upon reaching the castle, the horse snorted and stamped in front of the stables. I dismounted with some difficulty, rolling my ankle as I landed. With a hiss of pain, I crumpled to my knees, then stood tall, testing my weight. My ankle ached but held, and so I limped inside the barn. Peace enveloped me as I entered, welcomed by the scent of musk and hay. To my surprise, Pip waited at the door, and something about the stone creature made my heart turn. "You'll keep me company while we wait, won't you?" I asked.

He wagged his tail and followed me down the halls while various animals looked up at me. I caught my breath as a deer poked its head over the stall, unafraid as it munched on hay. The donkey was still there as well, staring at me out of condemning eyes, and above its head, white owls slept. A flash of red made me stop short, and when I peered over the stall, a red fox stared back at me, eyes like marbles. It twitched its pointed ears, and instead of fear, I only felt a sense of awe and wonder. Oren had once been a healer. Had all these creatures come seeking his help? Drawn to the haven he had created for them before sending them out to do his dark bidding?

Pain shot up my foot, reminding me of my ankle, and I hobbled to the workshop amid birdsong and the chatter of squirrels. I breathed in the scent of leather and wool, taking in the materials carefully stacked, as though the changes in the weather could not touch this. If this had been a true tailor's shop, they never would have kept the clothes where moths and rats could get at them. But I was grateful I'd come, for sitting in the workshop was more interesting than pacing in our room, waiting for him to return. At least I could amuse myself with a project, although something told me I'd have to wait a long time for Oren's return. He'd been honest, keeping me by his side, but now, once again, he'd pushed me away to disappear into a world I could not reach.

Wrapping my ankle to keep the pain at bay, I pulled out materials to make something, anything to keep myself occupied. And I was right. I cut and stitched and waited, but Oren did not return for days.

29. Oren

Once my horse carried Tanith away, I was alone with naught but the breeze to sustain me. I reached inside my cloak and pulled out the crystal pyramid Tanith had used to awaken me. She didn't know what it was. In fact, there were many things I hadn't told her—stories of my past, the lore of my people, the magic of the music, what eternal life truly meant and what would happen when the magic-thralls were free. We could go home. Not to this world full of mortals, corrupted by their greed and grasping fingers that reached for more and more because their lives were so short, so frail. But our true home, where I'd be freed from my duty. For now, I held up the pyramid.

It was a source of power given to me by the King of Hearts, only to be used in a time of dire need. It was never far from me, which was why it had been carelessly left on my coffin. I suspected the sorcerers back then assumed it was pure evil, a tool only I could unlock. In part, they were right. My power was devastating, too strong at times for even me to handle, so I had funneled it into the pyramid and used the flute to pull what I needed. I'd been cautioned against using it, but now, as I stood in the meadow holding the prism up to the light, I considered what I would wrought on this day.

Tanith's words about my strength and power had gotten me thinking. All this time, I'd relied on terror and fear to push Lord Faren to let the magic-thralls go, but it had not been enough. The citizens of Dowler were too frightened to strike back, to demand that he save their land. But if I took what was most precious to them, they would.

I closed my eyes, standing on the edge of a dangerous and difficult decision. I'd sent Tanith away so I wouldn't have to see the look in her eyes when I enacted my plan. Eventually, though, she'd find out. Would she forgive me? I suspected not, and that stayed my hand because with her, I'd come alive and with her was the potential of everything. I'd toss away a future with her if I moved forward with my dark plan. But it wasn't fair to the magic-thralls to force them to wait because I was falling in love.

My memory tunneled, taking me back to the dark times when I'd been caught and punished for wrong doing. Back in those days, I'd had great wings. I used to fly, soaring high above the clouds into the very heavens themselves. That sort of freedom was a rush of intoxication, and ever since my wings had been taken, I'd been forced to remain landlocked, flat-footed on the ground, moving slower than ever. A fair punishment for what I'd done, and yet, I'd hoped in time I might be forgiven, that I might regain my wings. Now I knew the truth of it. The past was gone, what's lost was lost, and now, I could only focus on the future. Which was why Tanith was so important. With her, the future wasn't all dark and gloom. It was bright and beautiful. In it, the version of myself I created would heal and mend and never cause destruction to rain down again.

I had to free the magic-thralls in order to get there, and the pain of what they were experiencing in the crypt was nothing compared to the pain I'd experienced when my wings were ripped from me. The bones that had held them to my back had been broken, sending sharp shards of pain into my spine. It took weeks to heal and every time I moved, excruciating pain had shot through my body, marring my vision, making me bend over, unable to eat or drink until I healed. During those days, I wished to die.

Anything to take me out of that pain. I imagined that was how the magic-thralls felt, caught in an endless cycle of torture, unable to die as they suffered pain, grief, and humiliation again and again. Well. No more.

The pyramid was pure power, enough to keep me asleep, enough for Tanith's blood to awaken me. Enough to give me the extra power I needed to ruin Dowler once and for all. Scraping the tip of the pyramid against my palm, I watched my blood cloud the crystal. It emitted a small sound, like the tinkling of bells.

Closing my eyes, I waited, allowing my power to build and grow. Unlike the river of blood, I would not collapse from using too much power here. I was awake, doing what needed to be done. No more games, no more delays. This was probably what I should have done first, but I had wanted to give the mortals a chance to repent, to see the error of their ways. But time after time, it had done nothing. Lord Faren was taking Dowler on a dark path, down which there would be no forgiveness. The most I could do was save the innocents, as Tanith requested. Although, after knowing her, I was sure she wouldn't see it that way.

I'd seen Lord Faren's household, the look of fear on his servant's faces, and heard Tanith's words, describing it as hellish. She thought I didn't know that they had abused her in that house, although she was strong enough to escape. So many weren't or had been blackmailed and blindsided, forced to comply with corruption. I suspected her aunt was one of those who suffered in silence, unwilling to end the cycle or stand up against Lord Faren. It was a generational curse, the abuse of magic, and their children would do the same thing again and again, unless I stopped it.

Time passed like nothing as I basked in my full power, standing like a tree firmly rooted against the coming storm. Black clouds rolled through, shutting out the light from the sun as though hiding the view of what would happen from those above. I was sure the stars winked out, unwilling to be silent watchers of tragedy. Taking my flute out, I lifted it to my lips and poured all of my power, anger, rage, and determination into a song.

Threads of it swirled around me, visible strings of silver and gold before twisting into a rope and shooting out. Even though my song was wordless, I heard the echo of the would-be words, calling, summoning. But this time, it wasn't my army I called. This time, those I summoned had no allegiance to me, no reason to come, which was why my song had to be strong, to overrule their desires for comfort and fear, to surpass their inclination to stay with those they loved and come to me.

I felt it the moment the first one answered, standing tall, eyes glazing over as if in a trance. I saw them in my mind as they trudged toward the invisible rope, as the song promised them their hearts' desire if only they followed it. Beyond the magic came shouts and wails as those who were found became lost, and those who were loved became empty shells. The people would never forget this day. This time, they would rise, and Lord Faren would have to set the magic-thralls free.

30. Tanith

I paced back and forth on the balcony, anger and abandonment in my every step. Fingers balled into fists, I crossed my arms and glared once again at the forest, the summer breeze making the trees sway and dance as though they were listening to some song. Oren had left me alone for three days, with only the animals in the barn and Pip for company. The cat had followed me into the castle once I was brave enough to go back to my room, badly in need of a bath. I washed and put on a bright red dress with crimson and lace. He still hadn't come and today was the third day, the day he'd promised to face Lord Faren and enact his terrible plan. What was it? Did he plan to leave me behind to ensure my safety, to protect me while he put himself in grave danger? I didn't want that, but he hadn't given me a choice.

Glaring at the trees—which really were dancing—I froze as a melody floated to my ears. No, it was a flute. *His* flute. A high, seductive song wafted from it, so enchanting my fingers loosened and I closed my eyes to listen. The notes of the song weaved through my mind and embedded themselves within my heart. The notes of the flute promised that all my secret hopes and dreams would come true.

Leaving the balcony, I ran out of the bedroom and down the stairs, Pip trailing at my heels as though I would run away—but I had no place to go. I paused on the second floor, and then dashed into one of the inner rooms and opened a window that overlooked the front of the castle. I leaned out, sure that Oren would come, sure that I'd see him at any moment. Indeed, his red hair blew in the breeze as he walked steadily, the flute in his hands. My jaw dropped as I stared at the unending line trailing behind him, hypnotized by his song.

Children. All ages, from toddlers careening on two feet to as old as Kinder. I sucked in a deep breath, my vision going dizzy as I covered my mouth with my hand. No. This could not be happening. This was the terrible thing Oren said he would do? Steal all of Dowler's children and bring them to his castle? Dumbstruck, I watched as he stopped in front of the doors and continued to play while line after line of children trailed into the castle. What would he do? Hold them hostage until Lord Faren gave in to his demands?

I recalled my younger self, my parents torn away from me, and the fear I'd felt at being alone in the world. Those poor children! Balling up my fists, I stepped back from the window, one thought resounding clearly. I had to stop him, beg him to return the children before this went much further. This was wrong. One did not take children away from their parents. No matter the cost.

Oren hadn't been terrible to me. In fact, after our nights together, I thought I might be falling for him. But once again, he'd shown me who he was, and that the tales weren't completely wrong about his nature. Cold. Cruel. Callous. Unafraid of anyone and anything, ready to go the distance if he believed others stood in his way. I recalled my words to him, acknowledging that he did nothing halfway. He always gave it his all, and that frightened me.

I raced down the stairs, reaching the entryway just in time to see the last child cross the doorstep, and I sucked in a deep breath, horrified to see that even Carter had fallen under the spell of the Piper.

"Carter." I hissed, hurrying to catch up. But his

eyes faced forward, and he walked automatically, deep under some spell I could not drag him out from.

Pressing a hand to my mouth, I stepped back while the melody whirled around me, tugging at my skirts, pulling me onward. Spellbound, I followed the music through the main halls, down wide staircase, past dark rooms lit only by candles, and into an underground hall. One by one, the children sat down, closed their eyes and went to sleep, while Oren stood in the middle, playing his hypnotizing tune.

When the last child was slumbering, Oren took the flute from his lips and stood still. A long moment passed as my anger shimmered. He lifted his head, amber eyes piercing mine as though he could read all the thoughts in my mind. "I know you do not approve," he said. "This is for good reason."

I marched up to him and slapped him across his perfect face.

Oren flinched. Quick as a flash, his fingers wrapped around my wrist. His gaze went to the slumbering children before he all but dragged me from the hall. It was old down there, smelling musty and sour. Almost—I shivered—like the vault underneath the palace where the magic-thralls lay trapped in torture. But to take the lives of children in exchange for them was hellish.

"You have to let them go," I snapped once we were out of earshot. "You can't steal children from their parents like that!"

He kept his tone even, his expression blank. "What do you think I'm going to do? Kill them?"

"Or spirit them away or something. You've stolen the future of Dowler and hypnotized them." My indignation gave way to fear and then horror. "What are you going to do with them?"

"There's a reason I did not tell you of this plan." Oren let go me and strode away.

I hurried to keep up. "Why?"

"Because you misunderstand my intentions. It was you who warned me about the innocents in Dowler, how unfair it was for them to suffer, and so I've removed them."

My jaw dropped, and I stared. "By stealing them from their homes and bringing them to your lair? Who will take care of them?"

"Their parents will, if they have the good sense to follow their children and flee. As I told you, there are tunnels beneath the castle, and the one that leads out was re-opened when the tower collapsed. If the people follow it, it will take them beyond the forest and leave them on a hillside. If they walk north, eventually they'll find a road that will lead them far, far away from here. It's the only way."

"Oh." Once again, I'd misinterpreted his intentions. With a sigh, I leaned against the wall, staring at him. At some point, I'd thought I'd figured Oren out, but he continued to surprise me. Taking the children was dangerous, reckless even, but if their parents followed and they were reunited, perhaps they'd forget the horror of being forced against their will to the Piper's doorstep.

"I did not have to do this." He fixed me with his piercing eyes. "But I suspect a fight will break out, and the city may not survive. Indeed, I don't believe anyone in Dowler should survive after turning a blind eye to such horrors. But that is the price of mortality. Fear. Maybe they will realize I have given them a second chance to do better. Instead of fighting evil, they let it into their midst."

"But you're the one they call the devil," I said softly.

"Yes." Moving closer, he slipped one arm around my waist, yanking me against him. He searched my face, and perhaps found what he was looking for, so he continued. "I've been called many names, often some form of devil because I make people pay for their actions. I force them to understand the consequences and no one likes that. But you've seen me at work, you've felt my magic, tasted my blood, you know I am no devil. That doesn't mean I'm good. As I once told you, I'm one of the Fallen. I used to have wings and live in celestial glory, but that time has passed."

"You were an angel?" I gasped, recalling the twin scars on his back.

He raised his eyebrows. "Another name, perhaps, but that is my past. This is my present and you, you could be my future."

He said the last words very low, as if he dared not speak louder. I closed my eyes, hearing them ring within my very soul. I'd been furious with him until he explained, and now I understood. The end was coming for Dowler, but he'd tried to save as many as possible. Because he'd left me alone for three days, my budding faith in him had wavered.

Pressing my hand to his face, I rose on my tiptoes, brushing my lips against his, and then held his gaze. "I'm sorry I doubted you."

With a sigh, he closed his eyes, soaking in my words, fingers threading through mine. "Tanith, the terms of our deal have been met. You are free."

Stunned, I stared at him. Blood rushed through my ears as I realized what he'd just said. I was free to go. I spluttered for words. "But … but you said the contract of our marriage was a life bond. How can you annul it?"

"I can't. But I keep my word. I made you a promise and I always keep my promises. You are free to go. I'd suggest you wait for the citizens to collect their children, then go with them through the tunnels. Forget Dowler, forget everything that happened here. Forget me. Start a new life."

How? The word crashed through my mind, and I felt as though someone had punched me in the stomach. I couldn't turn away. I couldn't run. Tears shone in my eyes as the truth of his words sunk in. "How can I forget you and everything that happened? You're my husband, we ..." I swallowed hard, blinking away the tears. "We consummated our marriage."

"We did," he agreed, his voice no louder than a whisper. "I've ruined you, haven't I?"

My voice rose as I protested, the lump of disappointment swelling in my throat. "I can't just walk away from this and forget you, forget I was married, forget the plague and magic and the flute and you ..."

"What are you saying, Tanith? Speaking plainly. I can't read your mind."

"No?" I yelled, as though he should have been able to. This was the opportunity I'd wanted ever since the idea of robbing the tomb sprang into my mind. Not only could I leave, but I'd be supported by the safety of numbers instead of alone. I could return to Solynn, start a new life, and perhaps Oren would even finance my journey. But the very idea of leaving him made my stomach clench, even though I certainly did not want to stay in Dowler.

When I did not respond immediately—because I was unsure exactly how to pinpoint and explain what I wanted—Oren went on. "I have to go. Time is wasting, and I want to strike while they are reeling in shock, before they have time to come up with a plan to strike back."

Letting go of me, he stepped away, and I took a step after him. "Wait, I'm coming with you."

31. Tanith

Oren did not try to stop me. He moved down the hall, boots ringing out, calling over his shoulder. “If you come with me now, you will miss your chance to leave with the citizens of Dowler. I will not be able to escort you to the city.”

“I understand,” I replied. Deep inside, I wondered exactly where he was going and why he wouldn’t be available any longer. Although it was none of my business what happened to Dowler after the magic-thralls were free. After all these decades, I could not imagine what terrible things they’d do with their newfound freedom.

I followed Oren to the double doors that led into the courtyard. He opened them wide, and a roar met my ears. Shouts and cries of angry parents. My eyes widened in alarm, catching sight of pitchforks glinting in the light. A crossbow sang and rotten fruit smacked into the door. A mob of villagers were at the doorstep and they had come for blood.

"We demand our children!"

"Give them back!"

"We know you took them!"

"You've taken everything else from us!"

"A curse on your house."

"Devil of Dowler!"

The angry yells of fear and hate rose. I waited for Oren to lift his flute to his lips, to quell them with his magical song. Instead, he opened the door wider, shielding me with his body, and stepped aside. When he spoke, his voice rose like thunder, and the shouts calmed like a storm being tamed. "Come. Take your children and leave this cursed city. If you value your life, you will go and not look back. And you will never return."

A pregnant silence extended of shock and disbelief. I found my courage and squeezed out from behind Oren. "Listen." I raised my hands. "I know I'm not one of you. I came from Solynn recently, and ever since my arrival, I've dwelled under the shadow of darkness that taints Dowler. My uncle, Lord Faren, has given in to evil ways and doom is coming to his house. It is time for him to pay for his deeds, to reap the consequences of his actions, but you have a chance to escape. Take the children and go through the tunnels. They lead to freedom where you can start life anew, free from the terrors that happened here. But I would caution you, remember Dowler, tell the tale to your children, and your children's children, so that they might remember there is a cost for wrong doing. That is why the Piper has come, not for vengeance and fear, not to punish you without reason, but to bring justice to those who have been wronged by the actions of my uncle, the priests, the sorcerers, and those who came before them."

"Who are you that we should listen to you?" An angry woman spat. "You're his wife, bewitched by him!"

Her vehemence was so potent, I stepped back as if she'd slapped me. "That may be so, but unlike you, I've lived with him," I retorted. "I've gotten to know the man behind the tales, the truth about who he is. Do you think for one moment that he would spare your lives, give you so many chances to flee, if he didn't have a heart?"

Low murmurs hissed, words that made my ears blush as someone pushed through the crowd. Up to the front came Aunt Matzie, with a bloody lip and a black eye swelling on her face. Uropa walked beside her, sporting a bloody lip of her own. I gasped at the sight, fingers tightening into fists. Lord Faren. He had not hesitated to lay his hands on me, nor did he hesitate to punish his wife. And for what?

The mob quieted down, and one voice rang out, "Lady Matzie, who did this to you?"

Facing them, she bowed her head, holding on to Uropa's hand for courage. "My husband, is not who you think he is." She proclaimed. "For years, our city has flourished because of magic. Dark magic practiced by the priests and the sorcerers. There are Others, like the Piper, slaves of magic who live in the mountain, their essence tortured out of them so that we might live in success. The Piper has come to help them, and we don't know what will happen once they are free. They might come after us, they might destroy this city and kill everyone who stays. I, too, was blind to all this, and choose to believe what my husband told me. But little by little, my eyes have been opened to the truth. We were wrong, and the Piper has done us a favor by taking our children. He has forced us to make a choice. To stay or to go. I've made my choice, and I've paid for it." She lifted her chin and touched her fingers to her bruised face. "I'm taking my children, and I'm going to start a new life, far, far from here."

With those words, she met my eyes. Arms wide, I went to her. The woman who'd been so quiet, so complacent through all of this, who'd argued in favor of Lord Faren, had finally seen the truth. Gingerly and awkwardly, she hugged me back. "Where are they?" she whispered.

Something cold and solid brushed my leg, and I looked down at Pip. Oh. Bending, I touched his head and then addressed my aunt. "This is Pip. He's a gargoyle, but he will lead you to the children. They are sleeping in a hall that leads to the tunnel. Follow it and you'll come out on the other side, far from here."

Her eyes widened slightly at the sight of the beast, but she showed no fear. After all she'd been through, it was likely nothing much surprised her. "Thank you, but Tanith, what will you do?"

I tilted my head up at Oren, who leaned against the wall, waiting. "I'm going with him to stop Lord Faren."

Pressing her lips together, she nodded. "Be careful. He's stopped torturing the magic-thralls, but I think he knows this is war, and he's preparing for something big."

"I understand, but Oren—the Piper—will stop him. I don't know if our paths will cross again, but regardless, go in peace."

"You too."

Pip led the way into the castle and the citizens followed, emboldened by the Lady of Dowler.

Oren took my arm and guided me through the throng of people, the air ominous with fear and tension and anger and rage.

The death horse waited for us outside the stable, but Oren opened the doors and peered inside. "It is time," he announced.

At first I thought he was talking to me, but then the creatures in the barn stirred, rising to their feet, stretching their wings, and I realized he spoke to his familiars, an army of creatures he'd once healed who owed their allegiance to him. They came when he called, they'd returned to help him, and now they came forth, to help this one last time.

Oren mounted the horse and pulled me up behind him. We thundered through the forest, the creatures racing behind us, and I wasn't sure if I'd made the right choice. Yes, I wanted to see this through to the end, but to face my uncle, the sorcerers, and the priests was more than I had bargained for.

When we reached the city, it was quiet. The people were gone, or if any had stayed behind, they hid in their homes. I saw what Oren had done to the glory of Dowler—buildings falling down and dead animals rotting in the street. Now and then, one of those hell dogs would rear its head, sending a shudder through me. This was not a place to live anymore. I shielded my eyes against the light as we passed the graveyard where it all began. To my surprise, Oren pulled the horse to a stop and lifted the flute to his lips, just as a ball of fire blasted out of the sky and arched toward us.

32. Tanith

Red balls of fire rained down from the sky, sizzling as they struck the ground around us. I screamed and ducked, but Oren had anticipated the retaliation. He played, the magic of his flute sending strands of gold into the air. I watched, astonished, for I could actually see each note as it burst from the flute, and the strings of music it left in its wake, flying up and off into the sky. Still, we weren't safe yet. As the fire rained down, Oren urged the horse into a steady walk, uphill to where the palace perched like a monster welcoming us into its lair.

As we approached, the sky darkened, clouds rolling across the sun, the light fading as fat raindrops poured out of the sky. Did Oren control the weather too? The fire fizzled under the rain, but it was too late for the houses and fields. They caught, burning steadily even as the rain came down, the scent of smoke filling my nose as I held tight to Oren.

When we reached the gates, the music ceased, and he dismounted slowly, his eyes holding mine, a determination in his gaze.

"This is where it ends, Tanith, and I will not relent. Will you turn back?"

I glanced over my shoulder at the city burning below. I tried to be brave even though my voice shook. "I think it's too late for that."

"Then stay by my side. The music will protect us as long as it can."

He held something up in his free hand. Flakes of gold glimmered, and I realized it was the crystal pyramid. I gasped lightly, recalling that fascinating relic he'd tossed in the air so lightly. I cupped my hands as he gave it to me.

"What is it?" I asked as the wind whipped up, embers floating like lightning bugs before the rain doused them.

"It is symbolic of life and death, and its power kept me sleeping until you changed the balance with your blood. This relic allowed me to access my true power. I did not understand how to use it until I sat on the hillock to think. Tanith, you gave me the gift of life, and in return, I will bring death to this city."

I held up the pyramid, staring at the golden flakes at the bottom. Some of them were turning black, or maybe their edges were charred? Perhaps I only imagined it. "Why give it to me?"

"Everything comes full circle and works together in harmony. Perhaps you were meant to enter the crypt, to steal from me, so that this could happen."

Then, without another word, he walked forward and began to play again. I followed as lightning split the sky and the clouds rolled darker. I should have been afraid, walking into the storm with the Devil of Dowler who wasn't so devilish after all. He'd come for retribution and revenge, he'd come to do what was right, to enact terrible justice, and I followed, blindly trusting in him, unwilling to consider why I stood tall in the face of danger.

The courtyard was empty, but upon the roof stood the sorcerers, chanting and weaving spells. Black and red words coasted in the air, and a vile scent carried through as they prayed to the sky. The balls of fire grew bigger, some almost falling on us, breaking the stones of the courtyard with the power of their impact. Embers stung my ankles, but I ignored the pain as Oren continued to play, and the ground shook.

A bellow of rage came from within the palace and the doors burst open. Sorcerers walked out, flanked by priests, their eyes dark, their faces tight with determination. The truth of the situation slammed into me, and I grabbed Oren's shirt, fisting it tight to give me confidence. The nasty truth lay before us. Many deaths would happen tonight. In fact, we might die too. But Oren did not falter, did not stop. His song swept through the air and the rain poured down harder. The balls of fire did not touch us and another roar filled the air. It was deeper than the hiss of the fire or the pounding of the rain, as bolts of light streaked across the black sky with the distant rumble of thunder.

Beneath the palace ran the river, in no danger of flooding the land. It was a beautiful sight to look at when the sun was shining and the waters glistened. But today it brimmed, overflowing, rising higher as though it sought the sky and magic pulled it there. The roar was the loud and deep voice of the river, and it was coming for us.

My hand on Oren's shirt trembled and then a cry tore out of the sky. Birds descended, sharp beaks out. Oren's familiars attacked.

It was chaos for a moment, all snarls and barks, wet fur and flesh burning. The music stopped and Oren whirled to me, almost dragging me up the steps into the hall. His hell dogs rushed by on each side, barking and leaping at the sorcerers who tried and failed to keep them at bay.

"Lead the way to the vault," Oren gasped.

I squeezed his hand and ran, ducking into the dark halls while the ground shook beneath us.

I knew the path by heart now, weaving through the dark innards of the palace. My heart thudded in my chest—go, go, go—and my feet gained speed. I ran while the roaring outside continued and the storm shook the building.

Just as we reached the temple, a loud cracking sound came, and we were hurled off our feet. I screamed as my knees skidded across the stone and the pyramid fell. Sucking in deep breaths to calm myself, I picked it up, cutting my palm on the sharp edges. A few drops of blood flowed out as Oren's arm came around my waist, lifting me. A curious light shone on his face, and that's when I saw the pyramid was shining. A golden hue blazed around it, as though the flakes within were burning up. The stain of my blood on the crystal evaporated, sinking into the light.

"Life and death," Oren murmured against my ear, and then we were running again.

The shaking grew stronger as we slipped into the temple, the incense braziers still burning, a sacrifice smoking on the altar. I turned my face away from the mutilated flesh and bone, even though it appeared to be an animal. The priests and sorcerers were nothing but monsters, there to suckle at magic and use it for their foul pleasure.

No one was within, yet I half expected them to be barring the doors that led to the vault. The mountain shook harder as we moved behind the curtain, and the stairs leading below were mere shadows. But the pyramid glowed brighter, the only light as we descended. The sickly smell of corruption, greed, sin, and torture made the air difficult to breathe.

"Here it is," I said, lifting the pyramid high to show off the doors to the vault.

A tug on my arm made me turn and Oren sank to his knees, face pale, hair damp with sweat. "I can't go in there," he whispered. "The magic forbids it."

33. Tanith

"Oren!" I cried, panic making my voice high.

He hunched over, wrapping his arms around his belly. Shaking his head, he spoke with effort. "This is the reason I've never been down here. It saps my strength and my magic is useless. Lord Faren has to give up the magic-thralls freely, he has to stop this magic. I'm sorry, Tanith."

Before I could respond, the doors to the vault burst open and my uncle walked out, flanked by three sorcerers. His hair was mussed, eyes red rimmed, and his fists bruised. Someone had struck him in the face, for his lower lip was swollen, and I couldn't help but hope that it had been Aunt Matzie, that she'd stood up to him at last, even though she'd escaped with a beating.

Lord Faren pointed at us. "I told you they would come, and look at the Piper now, weak as a kitten, barely able to hold up a finger. Take him into the vault and steal his magic. We'll put an end to this once and for all."

"What about the lady?" One sorcerer leered at me, fingers tapping together as he licked his lips, as though I were a tasty morsel.

I'd long suspected my uncle wanted to have his way with me, but he'd done nothing except use violence against me. I'd seen the guards and even the priests peek at me, but I'd kept my head down, ignoring their gaze. Now I feared what would happen in the crypt. Did the torture extend to more than mind games, more than tearing flesh from bone and blood-letting? Was this what the Others had to endure, and would endure longer because Oren could not save them? He went limp, and it took all three sorcerers to lift him.

Stunned, I watched as they dragged him inside, the silver light winking. The altar had been cleansed, waiting for him. What should I do? If I ran, I'd only dash into the arms of more sorcerers. Confirming my fears, my uncle's hand clamped down on my arm, dragging me inside. I didn't have my knife anymore, only the pyramid which glowed, almost burning hot in my hands. I glanced at Oren as they dragged him to the altar, trying with some difficulty to maneuver his limp body. He looked so sick, so deathly, even though he was one of the undying. If they tortured him, I could not take it.

I thought of Oren and his attitude toward me, the stolen kiss the night we'd wed, his calm control at my poor attempts to run away, the fury at which he'd protected me, and our frenzied lovemaking. My fear abated, followed by a surge of rage.

In one swift motion, I brought the pyramid up and drove the sharp end straight into my uncle's eye. He screamed, a terrible scream, and his flesh caught fire as the pyramid burst, sending a river of golden flakes down his body. His arms flailed as he moved backward, roaring and shouting in terrible pain. Crossing my arms, I watched, unable to tear my eyes away as the fire burned his skin, melting the flesh. It was only when white bone peeked out that I turned away and vomited.

Tears stung my eyes and when my vision cleared, the three sorcerers advanced toward me, as though I had some kind of magic they needed to devour. I backed away, pressing myself against the wall. I had nothing left to give as the mountain trembled, cracks opening on the walls and ceiling, steadily growing.

Lord Faren's last cries rang out, and then melted

away. As the sorcerers approached, a roar filled my ears and the mountain exploded.

Stunned, I cried out, reaching out to hold on to something, anything, to keep from being tossed away. My fingers found a rock, and I held as tight as I could as I squeezed my eyes shut.

The storm arrived to consume us, crashing into the mountain with a boom of rock and thunder. With it came the roar of wind, of water, the yipping of animals and the screams of the dying. It whirled around me as I held on, until my fingers ached and my body was sore from being battered through the storm.

It was a long while before it stopped, and when the silence came, I let go. I was soaking wet, lying weakly on a slab of rock like an offering the storm gave up. When I opened my eyes, it was cold, and a silver-blue light shone. I lifted my head, taking in my surroundings, and my heart lurched. The explosion had been so strong it had blown away the mountain and knocked the ceiling off the vault. The temple and palace were gone, and I stared up, up, up at the night sky far above me. The moon had come out, not quite full—the only light in the sky shining down on the bleakness below. Yet all around me was light, and that's when I saw them.

My limbs trembled as I sat up, taking in the boulders and slabs of rock around me. Walking among the ruins were the Others—feral, beautiful creatures, with pale skin and overly large eyes. Their skin was like starlight and they were tall, oh so very tall. They moved in unison, gliding toward one rock. They circled it, and that's when I realized they must be surrounding Oren.

I rose on my tiptoes, yet I could not see him. Was he alive? Unharmed? A sob rose in my throat and I swallowed it back, hugging myself, determined to be brave. This had been his plan all along, no? To best my uncle, to destroy his sorcerers, to cause the mountain to explode and destroy the magic that held the Others captive. For here, there was no oppression.

I stood there shaking, too afraid to move and ruin the moment as the Others walked free. They ignored me as they moved, their bodies all sharp angles, yet they still walked, despite what they had endured. A hush hung over the ruins until the music began, a pure, sweet note coming from within the circle. Oren played his flute, and if he played, he must be alive.

Weariness overtook me and I sank to my knees, not caring that I scrapped them on sharp shards of broken stone. The sweet melody filled the air. I closed my eyes and lifted my face, letting it sink into me. It was a song of beauty and hope, a song of overcoming, a song of freedom. The notes swirled around me, erasing the remnants of sin and evil and torture and corrupted magic. As I listened, a lightness filled me, and if I'd had wings, I would have lifted them up and flown away. The heaviness of the past was erased, the memories of darkness gone, and nothing remained but a future of hope and beauty.

My pulse slowed, and I opened my eyes as tears streamed down my cheeks. At last, the tears I'd held back for so long came. I wept for the death of my parents, the end of my life in Solynn, the corruption of Dowler, and even the fact that I'd been forced to kill my uncle. As my tears fell, the song washed away my guilt, my mistakes, and my grief.

This was a taste of creation, the song the Creator had sung when the world was called into being. This was beauty and hope and more, so much more than anyone ever deserved. A song like this could tame the world and cause people to bask in ethereal glory and beauty. A song like this could save a soul.

Silver light shone, brighter and brighter, as though the moon itself had come down and stood in our midst. My eyes widened as I watched the Others. Before my eyes, tiny wings sprouted on their backs. The music continued as their wings grew until they reached full maturity in a matter of moments. One spread her wings and turned.

When those pale eyes met mine, I gasped. It was the one I'd seen on the altar. Now, her skin was tighter, firmer, and although she was still naked, the marks of what she'd endured were gone. She gazed at me, expression solemn, and her words sounded in my head.

Thank you for finding the Piper. Thank you for setting us free.

She turned her face heavenward and leaped. Her wings came out to support her, and she shot straight up into the sky. One by one, each of the Others followed her, hands outstretched as they moved in a flash of silver light, flying higher and higher. I watched until they were out of sight, staring so long my eyes burned, because I could have sworn that they never disappeared. In fact, as they reached the sky around the moon, each one became a blaze of glory, a silvery star that filled the night sky in a plethora of splendor.

Awe-struck I watched, wishing I, too, could become a star in the sky, free in flight, free from this world, and free from the endless pain that humanity wrecked on each other. It was all so beautiful, I thought my heart would break from the glory of it, and even when they were gone, the light remained.

At last, my gaze left the sky, and I laid eyes on my immortal husband.

He perched cross-legged on the altar, which had shockingly remained intact through the storm. Wet hair stuck to his shoulders, his white shirt sheer. His haunted face was all hollows and angles as he took the flute from his mouth and met my eyes. Standing, he spread out his arms, as though welcoming me home. I went to him, almost ran to him, but the rock and rubble slowed me down.

The moment I was within reach, he dragged me into his embrace, crushing me against his body and kissed me until I was breathless. It wasn't merely a kiss, but relief and magic and weariness, all combined into one deep and desperate kiss. When he pulled back, his eyes blazed, and he trailed a finger down my cheek. "It is finished."

I nodded, having nothing to add to his words. The finality of them struck me, and a thread of unease left me wondering if there was a future for us. Still holding me, he pointed up. We stood in the crater of what was left of the mountain, and above us rose the waters, almost brimming.

"The river will fill this basin until it overflows, and the rock and rubble will cover this land. The city of Dowler is no more and will never be revived. It is nothing but a worthless ruin, a warning to those who would abuse magic."

My stomach twisted at the truth of his words.

He'd saved the citizens of Dowler from certain death, even though they did not deserve it. Those who had died here were those who perpetuated such evil—my uncle, his priests, and sorcerers. I thought of my aunt and hoped she would start a new life away from the rot of corruption. I wanted to ask what would happen now, but I was afraid to speak, afraid the future I wanted with Oren would be denied to me. So I nodded in understanding as the waters brimmed over, a waterfall pouring into the depths of the mountain. Soon it would fill. Soon we'd be washed away to our deaths.

But Oren held me tight. "Look at me, Tanith," he coaxed, drawing my eyes away from the deathly waters. "I'm not letting you go."

Arching his back, he stretched. A ripping sound rent the air as his shirt tore and wings sprung from his back. "Oren."

"Yes." He held my gaze. "I'm taking you home."

We rose, just like the Others, his wings bearing us upward. I wondered if we, too, would become like stars, to overlook the world, to bask in the heavens, where there would be no pain, no sorrow, no torture, no corruption. No more.

34. TANITH

Our flight into the night sky was cold, exhilarating, and terrifying. Oren flew with certainty, following a hidden path through the stars. I must have passed out while he carried me, for now I awoke to warmth, curled so tightly around Oren I couldn't see his face. A whiteness surrounded us and a blanket covered our naked bodies. I squinted, half afraid to open my eyes and break the spell.

"We're not dead, are we?" I whispered.

"No." Oren chuckled, his tenor tone stroking my inner fires. "We are alive. Would you like to see where we are?"

I loosened my grip on him, aware that one of my arms had gone to sleep. That probably wouldn't happen if we were dead. "Yes," I agreed, half sitting up. "Wait, no. I want to stay here with you in this warmth."

"It will be warm wherever we go, Tanith, it's summer."

I raised an eyebrow. "Yes, but it's always been summer."

He propped himself up on an elbow, leaning over me. "We are in the realm of the King of Hearts. His land has a true summer."

"What?" I squeaked and bolted upright, the blankets falling to my waist as I stared at Oren. I blushed as I realized we were both very naked. I wanted to explore that, but first, I needed answers. "The King of Hearts? Your friend from before? Oren, what happened back there? Your wings came back, and the Others flew away."

Instead of answering, Oren simply smiled and his entire face lit up. Peace enveloped him, a calmness I'd never seen. All the tension and angst from Dowler had left his body, making him appear younger. Rising, he pulled back the white curtains and handed me a robe. "Come, I will tell you all as I show you my home."

I slipped into the robe while Oren pulled on trousers. They hung loose around his hips and it was difficult to take my eyes off him, until he pulled the curtains back further, revealing the room.

"Oh," I breathed.

The white curtains surrounded the bed, which perched like an ivory cloud of comfort in the middle of the room. My feet sank into a plush carpet and on the walls crawled green vines and blooming red flowers. The open window let in the fragrant scent of lavender and roses and much, much more.

Oren threaded our fingers together, his grip warm and reassuring as he led me to the doorway. I sagged against him, pressing a hand to my mouth. A small sound escaped my throat as I stared. We were inside a charming cottage with ivy growing up the walls and vegetables hanging from the rafters. A fireplace filled one wall, with a round table in front of it. A shelf with books and other odds and ends sat tucked against the other wall, and a spiral staircase led upward.

It wasn't a grand palace, or an enormous castle with layers of halls and rooms and towers, and that's what I loved about it. It was tiny, cozy, and lovely in every way. "This is your home?" I gasped when I trusted my voice to speak without cracking. "Your true home?"

"There's more," Oren said quietly.

He led me to the front door, and I lost my voice again. The cottage rested on a hilltop and a valley descended below displaying vines heavy with grapes, golden daffodils blooming in the light, royal blue butterflies fluttering from flower to flower, and a gentle breeze with a hint of music within. I breathed deeply, taking in the floral tang and a hint of spice. Far in the distance, I thought I caught the winking towers of a castle, but I couldn't be sure.

When I spun to Oren, his gaze was on my face, drinking in my reaction. "Welcome home, Tanith," he whispered, cupping my cheek and kissing me oh so gently.

I closed my eyes, letting his caress linger on my lips. "This is wondrous. This is a paradise. How?"

"Wait, there's even more." Spinning me around, he led the way to the back door, which opened onto a patio.

Potted plants surrounded the cottage and a stone walkway led to a rose garden in full bloom. Beyond it, pine trees sloped into a forest, welcoming us to a secret haven. The music of water in the distance added to the charm and my heart swelled. Maybe we had died and our souls had been transported to a lush garden, for the colors were brighter than anything I'd ever seen, and the peace in the air left me with the sensation that nothing bad could ever happen here.

Oren led me outside to a shaded lounge. Leaning back against the pillows, he pulled me down beside him where we had a view of the cottage, the rose garden, and the plants waving in the breeze.

He was right. It was warm, and I tucked my legs under me, sitting so that I could study Oren's face. "Do you like it?" he asked, although he already knew the answer.

"Like it?" I gently punched his shoulder. "It's lovely and charming and beautiful and … it's really yours?"

"Ours now." He took my hand again. "Below us are the gardens of the King of Hearts, and these are his forests. He gave me cottage and garden as a gift, if I ever needed to rest. That was long, long before I was sent to Dowler."

Perhaps I really had seen a castle in the distance. Dowler seemed so foreign and far away from the warmth and beauty of Oren's home. "Will we meet him?"

Oren leaned forward, his eyes intense. "Tanith, here I intend to give you everything you want. We can go where you want to go, meet who you want to meet. If it is in my power, I will grant it, for you have given me everything."

"Oren I …"

"You don't know what you did, do you?"

I shook my head, squeezing his hand.

"You saved the magic-thralls."

My breath caught. "No, you did."

He shook his head. "The magic of the sorcerers made me weak, and you were strong. When you smashed the pyramid into Lord Faren's face, you brought down the mountain."

I shivered at the reminder. "I thought it was your plan all along."

"I had hope, and it was enough."

My throat went tight, recalling the desperation I'd felt in that moment. "What about the Others? Where did they go?"

"To their eternal resting place." Oren's gaze moved skyward. "They are the stars that shine in the darkness, accompanying the light of the moon. Their mortal bodies are gone, burned away in the filth from Dowler, and they will never feel pain again."

"I'm so glad they're free, Oren," I said softly, my heart swelling. "When you played that song and they changed, it was the most beautiful thing I'd ever seen or heard. They grew wings, glorious wings, and so did you. What happened to your wings?"

"Ah, they returned only for a moment, sparked by the song of creation to make all the broken things whole again. It allowed us to fly to the portal between worlds, back to this realm. I should have asked you, but Tanith, I couldn't imagine returning home without you."

"I'm glad." I leaned my face against the hollow of his neck and breathed in his scent. "When you told me I could leave with the citizens of Dowler and return to Solynn, I realized I didn't want that life anymore."

"No? What do you want, Tanith?" Bending his head, he slipped my robe off one shoulder and kissed my collarbone.

His lips on my bare skin sent a flutter of anticipation into my belly. When his hands drifted down to loosen the robe, I moved to straddle him.

Giving a dark chuckle, he pushed me down. "You haven't answered my question. What do you want, Tanith?" he murmured against my mouth.

"I thought it was obvious," I gasped, leaning back on my elbows as he settled himself between my legs.

He opened my robe and tugged it down my shoulders, then paused, trapping my arms behind me. A wicked glint danced in his eyes as he hovered above me. "I want to hear you say the words."

I licked my bottom lip, drawing Oren's gaze. Amber lust shimmered as his eyes raked down my body. Instead of touching me, he waited, keeping me on the edge. Rays of sunlight kissed my heated skin. My nipples peaked and ached, but it wasn't enough.

"You. I want you, Oren," I choked out, my voice high and breathy.

With a hiss, he crushed his lips against mine, and he tasted sweet like honey, the stain of darkness gone. When he broke the kiss, his jaw clenched. "Do you mean that?" he asked shyly. "Despite how we began?"

"I do."

With a shudder, he closed his eyes, basking in those words. "Even in my deepest slumber, I never imagined someone like you would ever love me, despite my past, despite our beginning ..." He trailed off, his hand closing around my hip, and for a moment I thought he'd cry, so overwhelmed. "I'd marry you again and make a promise to love you, protect you and honor you, no matter where life takes us." He kissed my shoulders and the swells of my breasts, making his way down my body as he spoke. "You've saved me in every way possible, and I adore you. I will do my best to deserve your love."

"Oren, you don't have to work for my love. You already have it."

He lifted my leg and rested it on his shoulder, his lips moving from my ankle up my thigh. "I've demanded so much from you. All I want is for you to be happy."

"I am happy," I assured him, squirming to free my arms from my robe. "Oren, what are you doing?"

"Kissing you."

His mouth was dangerously close to my core, and my stomach did an odd flip. "But not there."

"Yes, trust me, you'll enjoy it."

I tried to close my legs, aware that in the light's brilliance, nothing was hidden from his gaze. "But that's not …"

His eyes smoldered, demanding an answer. "Not what?"

"Not natural," I gasped, finally freeing my arms.

When I tried to sit up, Oren lifted my legs, spreading me wider. His tongue shot out and licked my core. A whimper escaped my throat as I lay back, surrendering to his feather light touch. The fluttering in my stomach coiled into pulsing need. I wanted him, desired him, needed him to fill me in every way, to take me over the edge of pleasure and let me fall, let us fall together.

"That's better," he murmured, licking me again.

I convulsed, spreading my legs wider, arching my back to keep his mouth there.

"I want to hear you scream and feel you go wild under my tongue," he said between licks. "You don't know what it does to me to watch you like this. You've never looked more beautiful."

"Oren," I gasped, my fingers curling into his hair as he moved deeper.

My heart pounded in my chest and blood rushed

to my ears as I gave in to the new sensations and the way he used his tongue. My muscles contracted around him, wanting more, deeper, harder, faster. When his tongue lashed my clit, I lost control.

I arched upward, unable to get enough air, enough of him, and pleasure slammed through me. I spasmed from head to toe, shaking so hard I almost knocked him off the bed. But Oren was with me, lifting me as his hardness sank into me. That thrust sent another wave of pleasure flowing through me, and I cried out as he kissed me, my scent on his tongue.

His thrusts came faster, and I pressed against his chest. My nails sank into his broad shoulders and he groaned against me as he moved. I rocked my hips up, meeting each of his thrusts with one of my own. Our sighs of pleasure grew louder, more frenzied as our movements intensified.

Pausing just for a moment, he lay back and pulled me on top of him without breaking our connection. I held his amber gaze as we moved as one. Bending my head, I kissed him, understanding at last what it meant to love and be loved in return. I had a long life ahead of me with Oren, and concerns about immortality faded away, because he was mine, I was his, and whatever future came, we'd experience it together. We had come through darkness to the light on the other side, and with love and magic, nothing would stand in our way.

We made love outside to the tune of invisible music, brought on by the wings of the wind. Perhaps if anyone thought of us, they'd assumed we'd died and gone to our eternal resting place. Where there was no sorrow or sadness or grief or misery.

I closed my eyes and held on to Oren's shoulders, letting the waves of pleasure wash over me again and again. And around us was nothing but light.

Thank you for reading *Lured by the Dusk*

If you enjoyed the tale and have a few minutes to spare, it would make my day if you would leave a brief review on the site where you bought the book. Just a few words on what you thought about Tanith and Oren would be perfect.

Leave a Review visit angelajford.com/products/lured-by-the-dusk

Exclusive Short Story

Don't miss this exclusive short story.

He's an immortal fae knight, she's a cursed warrior. To save their people from annihilation, they must go where the living have never gone before.

Every few years, the swarm comes, a terrifying pestilence that consumes the living. One sting from the deadly creatures brings not death but something much worse. . .

Every few years, Rainer, a fae knight sworn to protect the mountains, prepares his people to lose everything.

No one knows why the swarm comes, and no one can stop it.

Except for her.

Zelma is a warrior, sent to find the legendary firedrakes in the mountain. Instead, she's attacked by the swarm and left to die.

When she awakens in the hall of the fae knight, she's determined to continue her quest.

However, the sting has changed her, and new, frightening abilities awaken.

Afraid of becoming the target of the fae knight's wrath, she fights to control her magic as they travel into the heart of the mountains.

Will Rainer and Zelma save their people? Or will her magic kill them first?

Of Fae and Flame **is a complete, stand-alone short story set in the Nomadian universe.**

Only available at: https://angelajford.com/product/of-fae-and-flames/

Also by Angela J. Ford

Join my email list for updates, previews, giveaways, and new release notifications. Join now: www.angelajford.com/signup

The Four Worlds Series (epic fantasy)

A complete four-book epic fantasy series spanning two hundred years, featuring an epic battle between mortals and immortals.

Legend of the Nameless One Series (epic fantasy)

A complete five-book epic fantasy adventure series featuring an enchantress, a wizard, and a sarcastic dragon.

Night of the Dark Fae Trilogy (romantic epic fantasy)

A complete epic fantasy trilogy featuring a strong heroine, dark fae, orcs, goblins, dragons, antiheroes, magic, and romance.

Tales of the Enchanted Wildwood (fairy tale romance)

Adult fairy tales blending fantasy action-adventure with steamy romance. Each short story can be read as a stand-alone and features a different couple.

Tower Knights (fantasy romance)

Gothic-inspired adult steamy fantasy romance. Each novel can be read as a stand-alone and features a different couple.

Gods & Goddesses of Labraid (epic fantasy)

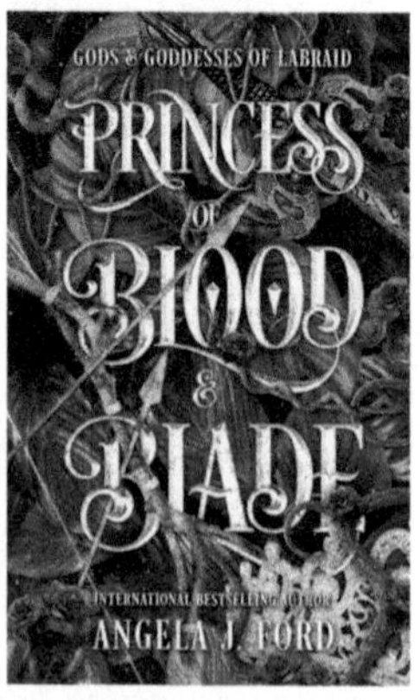

A warrior princess with a dire future embarks on a perilous quest to regain her fallen kingdom.

Lore of Nomadia Trilogy (epic fantasy romance)

The story of an alluring nymph, a curious librarian, a renowned

hunter, and a mad sorceress as they seek to save—or destroy—the empire of Nomadia.

Visit angelajford.com for autographed books, exclusive book swag and book boxes.

About the Author

Angela J. Ford is a best-selling author who writes epic fantasy and steamy fantasy romance with vivid worlds, gray characters, and endings you just can't guess. She has written and published over twenty books.

She enjoys traveling, hiking, and playing World of Warcraft with her husband. First and foremost, Angela is a reader and can often be found with her nose in a book.

Aside from writing, she enjoys the challenge of working with marketing technology and builds websites for authors.

If you happen to be in Nashville, you'll most likely find her enjoying a white chocolate mocha and daydreaming about her next book.

facebook.com/angelajfordauthor
twitter.com/aford21
instagram.com/aford21
amazon.com/Angela-J-Ford/e/B0052U9PZO
bookbub.com/authors/angela-j-ford

www.ingramcontent.com/pod-product-compliance
Lightning Source LLC
Chambersburg PA
CBHW070547310726
48982CB00011B/1488/J

9780578345192